Jack Higgins

Jack Higgins lived in Belfast till the age of twelve. Leaving school at fifteen, he spent two years with the Royal Horse Guards, serving on the East German border during the Cold War. His subsequent employment included occupations as diverse as circus roustabout, truck driver, clerk and, after taking an honours degree in sociology and social psychology, teacher and university lecturer.

The Eagle Has Landed turned him into an international bestselling author, and his novels have since sold over 250 million copies and have been translated into fifty-five languages. Many of them have also been made into successful films. The previous Sean Dillon novels are *Eye of the Storm*, *Thunder Point*, *On Dangerous Ground*, *Angel of Death*, *Drink with the Devil*, *The President's Daughter*, *The White House Connection* and *Day of Reckoning*.

In 1995 Jack Higgins was awarded an honorary doctorate by Leeds Metropolitan University. He is a fellow of the Royal Society of Arts and an expert scuba diver and marksman. He lives on Jersey.

JACK HIGGINS

EDGE OF DANGER

HarperCollins*Publishers*

HarperCollins*Publishers*
77–85 Fulham Palace Road,
Hammersmith, London w6 8jb

www.fireandwater.com

Special overseas edition
1

First published in the UK by
HarperCollins*Publishers* 2001

First published in the USA by
G.P. Putnam's Sons 2001

ISBN 978 0 00 783392 4

Set in Sabon by Palimpsest Book Production Limited,
Polmont, Stirlingshire

Printed and bound in Great Britain by
Clays Ltd, St Ives plc

To Tess,
who thinks it's about time . . .

IN THE BEGINNING

1

Paul Rashid was one of the richest Englishmen in the world. He was also half Arab, and few people could tell you which influence most ruled his heart.

Paul's father had been the leader of the Rashid Bedouin in the province of Hazar, in the Persian Gulf, and a soldier by both birth and tradition. Sent as a young man to the Royal Military Academy at Sandhurst, he had met Lady Kate Dauncey, the Earl of Loch Dhu's daughter, at a formal dance there. He was wealthy and handsome and, despite the obvious problems, it was a love match, and so, despite the initial misgivings of both sets of parents, they had married, Paul's father travelling back and forth between England and the Gulf as necessary. Over the years they had produced four children: Paul, the eldest, Michael, George and Kate.

The children were intensely proud of both sides of their family. In deference to their illustrious

Omani past, they all spoke fluent Arabic and were Bedu to the heart, but as Paul Rashid would say, their English half was just as important, and they fiercely guarded the Dauncey name and their heritage as one of England's oldest families.

The two traditions flowed together in their blood, the medieval British and the Bedouin, producing a general fierceness that was most remarked upon in Paul, and was perhaps best epitomized by an extraordinary incident that occurred when Paul was himself about to pass out of Sandhurst. He'd just gone home for a few days' leave. Michael was eighteen at the time, George seventeen and Kate twelve.

The Earl was away in London and Paul had gone down to Hampshire and found his mother in the library of Dauncey Place with a badly bruised face. She had reached to hug him and it was Kate who'd said, 'He *punched* her, Paul. That awful man punched Mummy!'

Paul turned to Michael and said carefully, 'Explain.'

'Travellers,' his brother told him. 'A bunch of them moved into Roundhay Spinney with four caravans and some horses. Their dogs killed our ducks and Mother went to speak to them.'

'You let her go alone?'

'No, we all went, even Kate. The men laughed at us, and then when Mother started shouting at them, their leader, a large man, very tall, very aggressive, punched her in the face.'

Paul Rashid's own face was very pale, the eyes dark, as he stared at Michael and George. 'So, this animal laid hands on our mother and you let it *happen*?' He slapped them both. 'You have two hearts. A Rashid's and a Dauncey's. Now, I will show you how to be true to both.'

His mother grabbed his sleeve. 'Please, Paul, no more trouble, it's not worth it.'

'Not worth it?' His smile was terrible. 'There is a dog here who needs a lesson. I intend to give him one,' and he turned and led the way out.

They drove to Roundhay Spinney in a Land Rover, the three boys. Paul had forbidden Kate to come, but after they left, she saddled her favourite mare and followed anyway, galloping across country.

They found the caravans parked in a circle, with a large wood fire in the centre, and a dozen or so men and women grouped around it, along with several children, four horses and dogs.

The large man described by the two younger

boys sat on a box by the fire drinking tea. He looked up as the three young men approached.

'And who might you be?'

'My family owns Dauncey Place.'

'Oh, dear, Mr high-and-mighty, is it?' He laughed at the others. 'Looks more like a prick to me.'

'At least I don't punch women in the face. I try to act like a man, which is more than anyone can say about you. You made a mistake, you piece of dung. That lady was my mother.'

'Why, you little shite . . .' the large man started, and never finished.

Paul Rashid's hand went into the deep pocket of his Barbour, and pulled out a *jambiya*, the curved knife of the Bedu. His brothers followed suit.

As the other men moved in, Paul slashed with the *jambiya* down the left side of the large man's skull, slicing off the ear. One of the other men pulled a knife from his pocket, and Michael Rashid, filled with energy he had never known, slashed sideways with his own *jambiya*, cutting open the man's cheek, sending him howling with pain.

One of the others picked up a branch and used it as a club to strike at George, but Kate Rashid ran from where she'd been hiding, picked up a rock and hurled it into his face with a shrill cry in Arabic.

As quickly as it had begun, it was over. The rest of the group stood warily, in silence, not even the women and children crying out, and suddenly the skies opened and rain poured down. The leader held a soiled handkerchief to his ear, or what was left of it, and groaned, 'I'll get you for this.'

'No, you won't,' Paul Rashid said. 'Because if you ever come near this estate or my mother again, it won't be your other ear you'll lose. It will be your private parts.'

He wiped his *jambiya* on the man's coat, then produced a Walther pistol from his pocket and fired twice into the side of the kettle over the fire. Water poured out and the flames began to subside.

'I'll give you one hour to clear out. I believe the National Health Hospital in Maudsley covers even scum like you. But do take me seriously.' He paused. 'If you and your friends ever bother my mother again, I will kill you. Nothing is more certain.'

The three young men drove away through the rain, Kate following on her horse. The rain was relentless as they entered the village of Dauncey and drove up to the pub named the Dauncey Arms. Paul braked outside, they got out and Kate slid off her mare and tied her to a small tree.

She stood looking at them in the rain, her face troubled. 'I'm sorry that I disobeyed you, brother.'

But Paul kissed her on both cheeks and said, 'You were wonderful, little sister.' He held her for a moment as his brothers looked on, then released her. 'And it's high time you had your first glass of champagne.'

Inside the pub were beamed ceilings, a marvellous old mahogany bar ranged with bottles and a huge log fire in the grate. Half a dozen local men at the bar turned, then took off their caps. The landlady, Betty Moody, who'd been polishing glasses, looked up and said, 'Why, Paul.' Her familiarity was expected. She had known all of them since childhood, had even been Paul's nurse for a time. 'I didn't know you were home.'

'An unexpected visit, Betty. There were some things I needed to take care of.'

Her eyes were hard. 'Like those bastards at Roundhay Spinney?'

'How on earth do you know about them?'

'Not much gets by me, not here at the Arms. They've been bothering people in the neighbourhood for weeks.'

8

'Well, they won't be a problem to anybody, Betty, not any more.' He placed his *jambiya* on the bar.

There was a sound of vehicles passing outside, and one of the men went to the window. He turned. 'Well, I'll be damned. All they shites be on their way out.'

'Yes, well, they would be,' Michael said.

Betty put down a glass. 'No one loves you more than I, Paul Rashid, no one except your blessed mother, but I do recall your temper. Have you been a naughty boy again?'

Kate said, 'The awful man attacked Mummy, he beat her.'

The bar was silent and Betty Moody said, 'He what?'

'It's all right. Paul cut his ear off, so they've gone away.' Kate smiled. 'He was wonderful.'

The silence in the bar was intense. 'She wasn't too bad herself,' Paul Rashid said. 'As it turns out, our little Kate is very handy with a rock. So, Betty, love, let's open a bottle of champagne. I think copious helpings of shepherd's pie wouldn't come amiss, either.'

She reached over and touched his face. 'Ah, Paul, I should have known. Anything else?'

'Yes, I'm going back to Sandhurst tomorrow. Could you find time to see if Mother needs any help? Oh, and excuse the fact that the child here is too young to be in the bar?'

'Of course on both counts.' She opened the fridge and took out a bottle of Bollinger. She patted Kate on the head. 'Get behind the bar with me, girl. That makes it legitimate.' As she thumbed off the cork, she smiled at Paul. 'All in the family, eh, Paul?'

'Always,' he said.

Later, after the meal and the champagne, he led the way across the road and through the graveyard to the porched entrance of the Dauncey parish church, which dated from the twelfth century.

It was very beautiful, with an arched ceiling and, the rain having stopped, a wonderful light coming in through the stained glass windows and falling across the pews and the marble gravestones and carved figures that were the memorials of the Dauncey family across the centuries.

Their peerage was a Scottish one. Sir Paul Dauncey it had been until the death of Queen Elizabeth, and then when King James VI of Scotland became James I of England, his good friend

Sir Paul Dauncey was one of those who galloped from London to Edinburgh to tell him. James I had made him Earl of Loch Dhu – the black loch or the place of dark waters – in the Western Highlands. As it usually rained six days out of seven, though, the Daunceys had understandably remained at Dauncey Place, leaving only a small, broken-down castle and estate at Loch Dhu.

The one signal difference between Scottish and English peerages was that the Scottish title did not die with the male heirs. If there were none, it could be passed through the female line. Thus, when the Earl died, his mother would become Countess. He himself would receive the courtesy title of Viscount Dauncey, the other boys would be Honourables and young Kate would become Lady Kate. And one day, Paul, too, would be Earl of Loch Dhu.

Their footsteps echoed as they walked along the aisle. Paul paused beside a lovely piece of carving, a knight in armour and his lady. 'I think he would have been pleased today, don't you?' He recited part of the family catechism, familiar to all of them: 'Sir Paul Dauncey, who fought for Richard III at the Battle of Bosworth Field, then cut his way out and escaped to France.'

'And later, Henry Tudor allowed him back,' young Kate said. 'And restored his estates.'

'Which inspired our family motto,' Michael added. '*I always return.*'

'And always have.' Paul pulled Kate close and put his arm about his brothers. 'Always together. We are Rashid, and we are Dauncey. Always together.'

He hugged them fiercely and Kate cried a little and held him tight.

After Sandhurst, Paul was commissioned into the Grenadier Guards, did a tour in Ireland and then in ninety-one was pulled into the Gulf War by the SAS.

This was ironic, because his father was an Omani general, a friend of Saddam Hussein's, who had been seconded to the Iraqi Army for training purposes and found himself caught up in the war as well, on the other side. No one questioned Paul's loyalty, however. For the SAS behind the Iraqi lines, Paul Rashid was a priceless asset, and when the war ended, he was decorated. His father, however, died in action.

For his part, Paul accepted the situation. 'Father

was a soldier and he took a soldier's risks,' he told his two brothers and sister. 'I am a soldier and do the same.'

Michael and George also went to Sandhurst. Afterwards, Michael went to Harvard Business School and George into the Parachute Regiment, where he did his own tour in Ireland. One year was enough, however. He left the army and joined a course in estate management.

As for young Kate, after St Paul's Girls' School, she went to St Hugh's College, Oxford, then moved into her wild period, carving her way through London society like a tornado.

When the Earl died in 1993, it was totally unexpected, the kind of heart attack that strikes without warning and kills in seconds. Lady Kate was now the Countess of Loch Dhu, and they laid the old man to rest in the family mausoleum in Dauncey churchyard. The entire village turned up and many outsiders, people Paul had never met.

In the Great Hall at Dauncey Place where the reception was held, Paul went in search of his mother and found one such person leaning over her, a man in his late middle age. Paul stood close by as his mother glanced up.

'Paul, dear, I'd like you to meet one of my oldest friends, Brigadier Charles Ferguson.'

Ferguson took his hand. 'I know all about you. I'm Grenadier Guards myself. That job you did behind Iraqi lines with Colonel Tony Villiers was fantastic. A Military Cross wasn't enough.'

'You know Colonel Villiers?' Paul asked.

'We go back a long way.'

'You seem to know a lot, Brigadier. That SAS operation was classified.'

His mother said, 'Charles and your grandfather soldiered together. Funny places. Aden, the Oman, Borneo, Malaya. Now he runs a special intelligence outfit for the Prime Minister.'

'Kate, you shouldn't say that,' Ferguson told her.

'Nonsense,' she said. 'Everyone who is anyone knows.' She took his hand. 'He saved your grand-father's life in Borneo.'

'He saved mine twice.' Ferguson kissed her on the forehead, then turned to Paul. 'If there's any-thing I can do for you, here's my card.'

Paul Rashid held his hand firmly. 'You never know, Brigadier. I may take you up on that some day.'

*   *   *

Being the eldest, Paul was selected to go to London to consult with the family lawyer about the late Earl's will, and when he returned late in the evening he found the family seated by the fire in the Great Hall. They all looked up expectantly.

'So what happened?' Michael asked.

'Ah, as you are the one who's been to Harvard Business School, you mean how much?' He leaned down and kissed his mother on the cheek. 'Mother, as usual, has been very naughty and did not prepare me.'

'For what?' Michael asked.

'The extent of grandfather's position. I never knew that he owned large portions of Mayfair. About half of Park Lane, for starters.'

George whispered, 'What are we talking about?'

'Three hundred and fifty million.'

There was a gasp from his sister. His mother simply smiled.

'And it gives me an idea,' Paul said. 'A way to put this money to good use.'

'What are you suggesting?' Michael asked.

'I did Irish time after Sandhurst,' Paul said. 'Then the Gulf with the SAS. My right shoulder still aches on a bad day from the Armalite bullet that drove through it. You did Sandhurst, Michael, and Harvard Business School; George a year in Ireland with One Para. Kate has yet to make her bones, but I think we can count on her.'

Michael said, 'You still haven't told us your idea.'

'It's this. It's time we banded together, made ourselves a family business, a force to be reckoned with. Who are we? We are Dauncey – and we are also Rashid. Nobody has more influence in the Gulf than we do, and what does the world want most from the Gulf right now? Oil. The Americans and Russians in particular have been nosing around the Gulf for months, trying to buy up exploration leases. But to get to that oil, they have to acquire the goodwill of the Bedu. And to get to the Bedu, they have to get through us. They must come to us, my family.'

George said, 'What are we talking about here?'

Their mother laughed. 'I think I know.'

Paul said, 'Tell them.'

'Two billion?'

'Three,' he said. 'Sterling, of course, not dollars.' He picked up a bottle of champagne. 'I am, after all, a very British Arab.'

*   *   *

With shrewd investment and the muscle of the Bedu behind them, the Rashids pushed the development of new oilfields north of the Dhofar. Money poured in, unbelievable amounts. The Americans and Russians did indeed have to deal with them, albeit unwillingly, and the Rashids helped Iraq restore its oil industry as well.

The first billion was realized in three years, the second in two, and they were well on their way to the third. George and Michael were named joint managing directors of Rashid Investments, and young Kate Rashid, now with her Oxford MA, became Executive Chairman. Any businessman who thought her simply a lovely young woman in an Armani suit and Manolo Blahnik shoes was swiftly disabused of the notion.

Paul himself preferred to remain a shadowy figure, behind the scenes. He spent much time in Hazar with the Bedu. To the Rashid, he was a great warrior, who would appear every so often to roam the desert by camel; to live in the old Bedu way in the Empty Quarter, guarded by fellow tribesmen burned by the fierce sun; to eat dates and dried meat with them.

Often he was accompanied by his brothers, or by Kate, who scandalized the locals with her Western ways, but no one could deny her, for by now her brother was a legend with more power than even the Sultan in Hazar, to whom he was a second cousin. It was whispered that some day he would be voted Sultan himself by the Council of Elders, but for now the old Sultan still held power, his chief strength the Hazar Scouts, a contingent of soldiers officered by British volunteers.

And then came the night when at an encampment at the Oasis of Shabwa as he was seated by a blazing fire, a Hawk helicopter came roaring in and settled in a cloud of sand.

Camels and donkeys milled around, children cried out in delight and women scolded them. Michael, George and Kate emerged in Arab dress, and Paul greeted them.

'What is this, a family reunion?'

Kate said, 'We've got trouble.'

He took her hand, led her to the fire and waved to one of the women to bring coffee.

Kate nodded to Michael. 'Tell him your bit first.'

Michael said, 'We've cracked three billion.'

'So we finally made it.' Paul turned. 'I'd be happier about it if I wasn't waiting for the bad news. Go on, Kate. I only have to look at your face to know if the weather is bad, and I'd say it's raining.'

'Have you seen the Sultan recently?'

'No, he's been on a pilgrimage to the Holy Wells.'

'The Holy Wells? That's a laugh. His only pilgrimage was to Dubai to meet with American and Russian government and businessmen. They've agreed on joint exploration rights in Hazar – without us.'

Paul said, 'But they couldn't possibly do it without Bedu cooperation. And they can't get that without us.'

'Paul,' Kate said, 'they can and they have. The Sultan's sold us out. You know how much the Americans and Russians have disliked dealing with us. Well, now they've cut us out. They're going to walk all over us – and walk all over the Bedu in the process. Without us, those damned oilmen are going to drill wherever they please, and the Arabs can go to hell.'

Paul said, 'Is this true, Michael?'

Michael nodded. 'They are going to rape the desert, Paul. And there's not a damned thing we can do about it.'

Paul nodded thoughtfully and stirred the fire. 'Do not speak in haste, Michael. There are always things that can be done – if one has the will.'

'What do you mean?' George asked.

'Not now,' said Paul. He turned to Kate. 'Do you have the Gulfstream at the air force base in Haman?'

'Yes,' Kate said.

He drew her up and kissed her on the forehead. 'Have a good night. Tomorrow we will speak.'

He nodded to his brothers, and they all rose. Kate turned and began to walk away, and it was then that it happened. Beyond, from the shadows, a Bedu emerged screaming, a curved *jambiya* raised above his head, running straight at them, with Kate in his way. Paul's guards were caught momentarily unaware, their AK-47s at their feet, coffee cups in their hands, and it was Paul Rashid who flung himself forward, knocked his sister to the ground and pulled a Browning from his waistband. He fired four times quickly and the assassin was driven to the sand.

There was another shrill cry and a second man, *jambiya* raised, emerged from the darkness, but this time he was instantly overwhelmed by the guards.

'Alive!' Paul called in Arabic. 'Alive!' He turned

to George. 'Who is he, where does he come from – find out.'

George ran to the struggling group as they held the man down, and Paul helped Kate up. 'Are you all right? You're not harmed?'

She held him close and spoke in Arabic. 'No, my brother, thanks to you.'

He embraced her. 'Leave this to me. Go to bed.'

She turned reluctantly and Paul Rashid went into the shadows and squatted beside the second assassin, now pegged out on the ground. The man's face was lined and drawn. The pupils of his eyes were like pinpricks and there was foam around his mouth.

'A hired assassin drugged with *quat*,' George said.

Paul Rashid lit a cigarette and nodded. *Quat* was a narcotic found in the leaves of shrubs in Hazar. Many of his people were addicted to it. For some, it lent false courage.

For this man, it would lend only death.

'Do what you have to do,' he said to George.

He went back and sat by the fire, drank more coffee, and Kate appeared and sat at his side. A cry of pain came from the shadows, a sudden scream, then silence. George and Michael appeared.

'So?' Paul asked.

'The Sultan arranged it for the Americans and Russians. They couldn't afford us staying alive.'

'What a pity for them,' Paul Rashid said, 'that they failed.'

There was a pause. Michael and George sat down. 'What happens now?' George asked.

'First, I think it's time for a new Sultan. Your speciality is working with our people in Hazar,' Paul told him. 'See to it. But there's a larger issue at stake. Do we let these mighty powers do this to our people? Do we let them destroy our land? Do we let them strike at *us*? No, I think we must strike at them.'

At that moment, his mobile phone rang. He took it from his robe. 'Rashid.'

He sat there in the firelight and his face changed before them, his eyes turning to bleak holes.

He said, 'We'll be there as soon as possible.'

He switched off the phone and handed it to Kate. 'Call Haman. Tell them to have the Gulfstream ready for immediate departure. We're leaving in the helicopter now.'

'But Paul, why? What happened?' Kate demanded.

'That was Betty Moody. Something terrible has happened to Mother.'

2

Something terrible indeed. Driving home to Dauncey Place, Lady Kate had been involved in a head-on collision with a car driving on the wrong side of the road. The Rashids made it to the hospital ten minutes before she died, time enough only to stand, the four of them, and hold her hands.

'My lovely boys,' Lady Kate said in her bad Arabic, always the family joke. 'My gorgeous girl. Always love each other.' And she was gone.

Michael and George broke into a storm of weeping, but not Kate. She clutched Paul's hand as he leaned down to kiss his mother's forehead and her eyes burned, but there were no tears. Those would come later – after she discovered the man responsible for this.

But when the name came, there was only more bad news. A Chief Inspector of the Hampshire Police told them that, yes, the other driver, one

Igor Gatov, had been driving on the wrong side of the road on his way to London from Knotsley Hall, which was owned by the Russian Embassy. And, yes, he had most certainly been drunk, and miraculously had been able to walk away from the crash with only minor injuries. But unfortunately, he was also a commercial attaché at the Russian Embassy in London, which meant that he had diplomatic immunity. Their mother's killer could not be tried in an English court.

In deference to their mother's Christianity, they buried her in the mausoleum at Dauncey village church on a March afternoon. One of the most important Imams in London graced the proceedings with his presence and, standing there, the three Rashid brothers and young Kate had never felt closer.

Later, at the reception in the Great Hall at Dauncey Place, Paul Rashid was approached by Charles Ferguson. The Brigadier said, 'This is a rotten business, Paul. I'm so sorry. She was a great lady.'

Kate said, 'Do you know something you're not telling us, Brigadier?'

Ferguson looked at her. 'Give me a call sometime.'

He walked away. Kate said, 'Paul?'

'As soon as we're done here,' her brother said, 'we'll go and see him.'

Two days later, Paul and Kate Rashid arrived at Charles Ferguson's Georgian flat in Cavendish Place, London. They were admitted by Ferguson's Gurkha manservant, Kim, and found that Ferguson was not alone. Two other people were there, one of them a small man, his hair so fair that it was almost white.

'Lady Kate, this is Sean Dillon, who works for my department,' Ferguson said, then introduced the other, a red-haired woman. 'Detective Superintendent Hannah Bernstein from Special Branch. Lord Loch Dhu, how can I help? May we offer you a glass of champagne?'

'No, thank you. My sister perhaps, but I would prefer a Bushmills Irish whiskey like the one Mr Dillon is pouring.'

'Good man yourself,' Dillon told him, 'but first, the ladies,' and he poured champagne.

Hannah Bernstein said to Kate, 'You went to Oxford, I believe? I was at Cambridge myself.'

'Well, that's not your fault,' Kate said and gave a small smile.

Her brother said, 'I did Irish time, with the Grenadier Guards and the SAS. I heard many things about Sean Dillon there.'

'Probably all true,' Hannah Bernstein told him, with an undertone Rashid could not decipher.

'Don't listen to her,' Dillon said. 'I'll always be the man in the black hat to her, but to you and me, Major, to soldiers everywhere, we're the men who handle the crap the general public can't. That's a showstopper,' Dillon added and turned to Kate. 'Wouldn't you agree that's a showstopper?'

She wasn't in the least offended. 'Absolutely.'

'So,' Paul Rashid said, 'Igor Gatov, a commercial attaché at the Russian Embassy, kills my mother while driving on the wrong side of the road, drunk. The police say he has diplomatic immunity.'

'I'm afraid so.'

'And he's gone back to Moscow?'

'No, he's needed here,' Ferguson told him.

'Needed?' Rashid asked.

'The Secret Security Services would not thank me for telling you this, but they're not my best friends. Tell him, Superintendent.'

'But how far do I go?' she asked.

'As far as it takes,' Dillon said. 'This Russian shite takes out a great lady and walks away.' He poured another Bushmills, toasted young Kate, turned to Paul Rashid, and said in good Arabic, 'Gatov is a dog of the first water. If the Superintendent hesitates, don't hold it against her. She has delicate sensibilities. Her grandfather is a rabbi.'

'And my father was a sheik,' Paul Rashid said to her in Hebrew. 'Perhaps we have much in common.'

Her surprise was obvious. 'I'm not sure what to say,' she replied in the same.

'Well, I am,' Dillon cut between them in English. 'It's not just the Russian Embassy that's keeping Gatov from justice. There's the American connection.'

There was a pause. 'What would that be?' Paul Rashid asked.

Hannah said to Rashid, 'As you know, the Americans and Russians are great rivals in southern Arabia, but they will work together if it suits them.'

Paul said, 'I know all this, but what has it to do with my mother's death?'

It was Dillon who told him, and in Arabic. 'This piece of dung is a double agent. He worked for the Americans on the other side of the coin. It's not only the Russians who don't want him in court, but the Yanks as well. He's too important.'

'Too important for what?' Paul Rashid asked.

It was Ferguson who said, 'The Americans and Russians are working on some kind of oil deal – and Gatov was brokering it. He's right in the middle. There are billions to be made down there.'

Dillon said, 'He's right. Arabia Felix, Happy Arabia, that's what they called it in the old days.'

Kate Rashid, who had listened in silence, said, 'So we're talking about money here?'

'I'd say so,' Dillon said.

'And to facilitate their wheeler-dealing, both the Americans and Russians look upon my mother's death simply as an inconvenience?'

'A severe one.'

She paused and glanced at her brother, who nodded. She said, 'Some days ago, at the Oasis of Shabwa, an interesting event took place. Were you aware, Brigadier, that the Sultan of Hazar had allied himself not only with a major American oil company but also a Russian one?'

Ferguson frowned. 'No, that's news to me.'

'Two assassins attempted to kill my brother on the night we received news of my mother's accident.' She nodded to Dillon. 'One tried to kill me. My brother saved my life and shot him dead.'

'The important thing is that we discovered from the second assassin that I was targeted by the Sultan himself on behalf of the Americans and Russians,' Paul Rashid told them.

Ferguson nodded. 'He told you everything?'

'Of course,' Dillon put in.

Ferguson said, 'Are you suggesting that your mother's death was deliberate?'

'No,' Paul said. 'The police have gone over the evidence with us, and I see nothing these dogs could have gained by murdering my mother. But what is clear to me is that, for them, life is cheap. And I plan to make it very expensive.'

He stood up and held out his hand. 'Thank you very much for your information, Brigadier.' He turned to Dillon. 'In the Guards in South Armagh, a Loyalist politician told me once that Wyatt Earp could account for the deaths of twenty men, but that Sean Dillon didn't even know his total.'

'A slight exaggeration,' Dillon told him. 'I think.'

Rashid smiled at each of them and turned to follow Kim. Kate held out a hand to Dillon. 'You're a very interesting man.'

'Oh, you have a way with the words, girl dear.'

He kissed her hand. 'And a face to thank God for.'

'That's my sister, Mr Dillon,' Rashid said.

'And how could I forget it?'

They left, and before Ferguson could say anything, his red phone rang. He picked it up, listened, had a brief conversation, then replaced the receiver, his face grave.

'It would seem the Sultan of Hazar has just been assassinated.' He turned to Dillon. 'A remarkable coincidence, don't you think?'

The Irishman lit a cigarette. 'Oh, yes, remarkable.' He blew out smoke. 'I know one thing. I feel sorry for Igor Gatov.'

That evening, there was a function at the Dorchester, a political affair attended by the Prime Minister, and Ferguson, Bernstein and Dillon had been drafted for security, not without a little grumbling.

Dillon and the Superintendent moved in from the Park Lane entrance to the ballroom, checked all the arrangements and, satisfied, followed Ferguson through. And there at the bar was the Earl of Loch Dhu and his sister.

Ferguson said, 'Talk about a bad penny. Hannah and I will continue with the security. See if there's anything more you can find out, Dillon.'

Kate and Paul Rashid stood together, watching the crowd, as Dillon approached and said, 'What a coincidence.'

'I've never believed in coincidences, Mr Dillon,' Paul Rashid told him. 'Have you?'

'Funny you should say that. Like you, I'm a cynic, but today –'

Just then, a young man interrupted. 'My Lord, the Prime Minister would like a word.'

Rashid said to the Irishman, 'I'm so sorry, Mr Dillon, our conversation will have to wait. However, I'd appreciate it if you'd see to my sister for me.'

'It'd be an honour.'

Rashid walked away and Kate turned to Dillon. 'Well, as long as you're seeing to me, how about a fresh drink?'

Dillon was just turning to hand her a glass when a rather large man with a florid face appeared, and gave her a squeeze from behind. 'Kate, my darling,' he said in a booming voice.

Seeing he would have no chance to talk to her now, Dillon decided to leave – but managed to step on the man's right foot as he moved away. The man let her go. 'Damn you, you clumsy oaf.'

Dillon smiled. 'So sorry.' He bowed to Kate. 'I'll be in the Piano Bar.'

He walked through the main hotel to the Dorchester's Piano Bar, where, since it was still early evening, it was quiet. Guiliano, the manager, greeted him warmly, for they were old friends.

'Glass of champagne?'

'Why not?' Dillon said. 'And I'll give you a tune on the piano while you're waiting for your man to turn up.'

He was well into a Gershwin melody when Kate Rashid appeared.

'I see you're a man of many talents.'

'Good barroom piano is all it is, ma'am. What happened to the gentleman?'

'The gentleman – and I use the term loosely – is Lord Gravely, a life peer who inhabits the House of Lords and does little good there.'

'I wouldn't think your brother would welcome his attention to you.'

'That's an understatement. Did you really need to stand on his foot?'

'Absolutely.'

'Well, I'm glad. The man is an absolute pig. He's

always grabbing at me, groping me. The man just won't take no for an answer. He deserves a sore foot, and a lot more besides.'

She picked up his glass of champagne and finished it off. 'Anyway, I just came by to say thank you. Now I'd better be off. I asked for my car at seven.'

Seeing that there was to be no further conversation, Dillon smiled. 'It's been a sincere sensation.'

She walked out and Dillon came to the end of his tune and decided to follow her. He didn't know why exactly, but there just seemed to be unfinished business.

He went out of the main door, turned right into Park Lane and found limousines picking up people from the reception at the ballroom entrance. Lady Kate Rashid was standing on the pavement, a shawl about her shoulders, and there, suddenly, was Lord Gravely again. He put his arm around her and pulled her close, whispering in her ear. She struggled and two things happened simultaneously. Paul Rashid's Daimler coasted in to the kerb, with Rashid in the back, and as he scrambled out Dillon moved in on Gravely and screwed both fists into his kidneys. Gravely cried out and released Kate, and her brother pulled her away into the car. Gravely turned on Dillon in a fury and, pivoting, Dillon gave Gravely a reverse elbow strike to the mouth, whereupon his lordship slid down to the pavement.

As they were driven away, Rashid looked out of the rear window and saw Dillon melt into the crowd and a policeman approach Gravely. 'A remarkable man, Dillon. I owe him one. Are you all right?'

'I'm fine, brother, and I'm the one who owes him.'

'You like him?'

'Very much.'

'I'll have him checked out thoroughly.'

'No, Paul, that I'll do for myself.'

After a lawyers' meeting the following morning, the two of them drove down to Dauncey Place. Paul had phoned ahead, so his brothers were there as well, and they'd given photos of Gatov to Betty Moody. Betty in turn had spoken to the locals.

When he saw her in the bar that evening, she gave him his usual glass of champagne and spoke in a low voice.

'He's in the village, Paul, arrived at lunchtime with a party from the Russian Embassy.'

'Good.' He savoured the champagne.

'What are you going to do?' she asked.

'I'm going to execute him, Betty,' he told her and smiled over her sharp intake of breath.

Later that night, he spoke to his brothers in the Great Hall. Betty was there as well – she'd come up from the pub with last-minute information overheard from the local staff at Knotsley Hall: Gatov was leaving at eleven to drive overnight to London.

Paul Rashid told his brothers what he intended to do, but he'd purposely excluded Kate. 'I don't want her involved,' he said. 'This is men's work.'

What he did not know was that Kate was on the minstrel gallery above, and listening. Furious, she was about to call out, but Betty appeared behind her and fastened a hand on her shoulder. 'You mind your manners, girl. Your brothers are going in harm's way. They don't need you making it difficult for them.'

And Lady Kate Rashid, for the moment a child again, did as she was told.

*　　*　　*

35

That night, Igor Gatov drove around a corner of a narrow country lane and found a van tilted into a ditch and someone lying in the middle of the road. He got out of his BMW, walked forward and leaned over the figure on the ground. It was Paul Rashid, and he struck him across the neck.

He and his brothers wore black Special Forces overalls. Michael and Paul carried the semiconscious Gatov to the BMW and pushed him behind the wheel.

George went to the van, got in and reversed it out of the ditch. Paul Rashid took a bottle from his overalls and doused Gatov in petrol.

'Fire purifies, so the Koran tells us,' he said, then switched on the engine of the BMW and slipped off the handbrake. 'It's not much of an exchange for my mother, but it's better than nothing.'

He flicked his lighter, touching the edge of Gatov's petrol-soaked jacket, which immediately started to burn. Then George and Michael pushed, and the BMW rushed down the hill and hit the end of an old stone bridge, where it fireballed.

The next morning, at the Ministry of Defence, Hannah Bernstein took a signal flimsy to Ferguson in his office. It detailed the terrible accident that had burned Igor Gatov to death.

'Dear me,' Ferguson said. 'Another remarkable coincidence.'

Sean Dillon leaned against the door and lit a cigarette. 'The question is – what coincidence is going to be next?'

Sitting in the drawing room of Kate's house in South Audley Street, Paul Rashid said, 'Gatov is dead. The Sultan is dead. Such executions are right and just. But they are not enough.'

Michael said, 'What do you mean, brother?'

'I mean it is not enough simply to have eliminated two small men. Their deaths will quickly be swallowed up and the great powers will continue to swagger arrogantly around the world as if nothing has happened. America and Russia, the two Great Satans, have attacked Arab culture, they have walked over the Bedu, they have screwed Arabia and Hazar out of what is rightfully theirs – and ours. We must teach them a lesson they will never forget.'

'What do you have in mind?' asked George.

'First: Kate. I want you to contact our friends in

the Army of Allah, the Sword of God, Hizbullah, everyone. I want them screaming about the US and Russia trying to plunder Arabia. I want them creating havoc whenever and wherever possible.'

'Then what?' said Michael.

'Then we assassinate the President of the United States.'

There was a stunned silence. Michael said in a whisper, 'But why, Paul?'

'Because Gatov was just a servant. Because the Sultan was just a pawn. Because it is no good killing just the little people. If we don't make a statement – and I mean a *big* statement – the great powers will never understand. They will never leave us alone. Properly orchestrated, the killing of President Jake Cazalet will tell the world once and for all that Arabia is for the Arabs. For Cazalet, the buck stops here – isn't that what they say? Oh, we could kill the Russian Premier instead – he's just as culpable – but Cazalet will make a much bigger impact.'

There was more silence. Michael said, 'You're serious about this?'

'Yes, Michael. Never more serious. It is time to take a stand.' He looked hard at him. 'This is for the Bedu.' He shifted his eyes to George. 'This is for Hazar.' He rested his gaze on Kate, and they sat, their eyes locked, for what seemed like minutes. Finally, 'This is for Mother.' The harsh whisper seemed to fill the room.

After a moment, Kate said, 'But who will attempt this thing?'

'A mercenary. With the peace process taking over Northern Ireland, there are many expert IRA killers at loose ends.' He produced an envelope and passed it to her. 'This man, one Aidan Bell, comes highly recommended. He is to be found in County Down. It seems he shot a Russian general for the Chechens, and blew up his staff. A man willing to take risks. Go and see him, Kate. Take George with you. He's soldiered over there and knows the ropes.'

There was no longer any hesitation. A decision had been reached. 'Of course, brother.'

'One other thing.' He lit a cigarette. 'You liked Sean Dillon?'

'I told you.'

'Go and see him. Arrange an accidental meeting. Concoct a story. See what he knows of Aidan Bell.'

She smiled. 'It'll be a pleasure.'

'Well, don't make it too much of one.' He smiled back at her.

LONDON

COUNTY DOWN,
NORTHERN IRELAND

3

Kate Rashid went through the information her brother had supplied and it was good, detailed stuff. Aidan Bell was forty-eight years of age, had been a member of the IRA since the age of twenty, and had never served a day in prison. For years, he'd been a member of the Irish National Liberation Army, a very extremist organization. He had often been at loggerheads with the Provisional IRA but was responsible for some important hits.

The most interesting fact was that over the years, he had also worked as a mercenary, cash on the nail, for many foreign revolutionary movements.

Kate put the matter into the hands of her head of security at Rashid Investments, a trusted man and ex-paratrooper named Frank Kelly. Not in complete detail, however. She didn't trust any employee that much. At this stage, all she wanted was a chance to meet Dillon as if by chance, and it came on the following Monday night.

Kelly phoned her at the South Audley Street house, which was only five minutes up the road from the Dorchester. 'Dillon has just gone into the Piano Bar. He seems dressed for a night out, got a dark blue suit on and a Guards tie.'

'But he wasn't in the Guards.'

'Probably taking the piss, if you'll excuse my language, ma'am. I did a lot of Irish time in One Para. I know about this guy.'

'I didn't realize you were in One Para, Kelly. Did you know my brother George?'

'Yes, ma'am, though he was way above me. He was a Second Lieutenant, and I was just a Sergeant in my day.'

'Fine. Have you a car there?'

'One of the company Mercs.'

'Drive up and get me. You can come to the Dorchester and wait. You personally, Kelly. I don't want anyone else.'

'Lady Kate, I wouldn't dream of making it any-one else,' Kelly told her.

He picked her up, a well-dressed man no more than five-feet-eight, with a good, hard face and hair close-cropped, the Army bit that wouldn't go away. In no time, he had dropped her at the Dorchester and parked in one of the privileged spaces.

She went through the swinging doors, trim in a black trouser suit. As she walked into the bar, there was music, and there was Dillon playing the piano again.

Guiliano turned up. 'Lady Kate, what a pleasure. The usual table?'

'No, the bottom left by the piano. I'd like to speak to the pianist.'

'Ah, Mr Dillon. He's good, isn't he? Sits in before our regular comes, only now and then. Lord knows what he does the rest of the time. You know him?'

'You could say that.'

He escorted her to the table. She nodded to Dillon, ordered a glass of Krug champagne, sat down, and took out her mobile phone, which was strictly against bar rules. She called her brother George at his apartment not too far away.

When he answered, she said, 'I'm in the Piano Bar at the Dorchester. Dillon is here and Frank Kelly is outside. Call him on his mobile, and tell him to pick you up. I want you.'

'Of course,' George said. 'See you soon.'

Dillon was really very good, she decided. He was playing the old standards, the kind of things she liked. A cigarette dangled from the corner of his mouth and he suddenly moved into 'Our Love Is Here to Stay', a slightly crooked grin on his face. As he came to the end, the regular pianist appeared and Dillon smiled, slid off the piano bench and the other man took over.

The Irishman came across to her. 'Serendipity, isn't that the word? This is a total and unexpected pleasure.'

'Why, Mr Dillon, you're a man of erudition.'

'Well, unlike you, I didn't go to Oxford. I had to make do with the Royal Academy of Dramatic Art.'

'You were an actor?'

'Oh, come off it, Kate Rashid, you know damn well what I was, all of it.'

She smiled, and as Guiliano came up she said, 'His personal preference used to be Krug, but I understand he's switched to Louis Roederer Cristal. We'll have a bottle.'

Dillon produced a silver cigarette case, opened it and took one out. She said, 'You might ask a lady,' reached, took the case from him, examined it and selected a cigarette herself. 'Art deco. A man

46

of taste. Or perhaps a souvenir of the National Theatre?'

'You are well informed,' Dillon said. He flicked his Zippo and gave her a light as the champagne arrived. He lit his own cigarette. 'You know, there's coincidence, which could be this meeting, and then there's Carl Jung.'

'You mean synchronicity? A deeper motivation is intended?' He toasted her. 'So what are we into here?'

At that moment, George came down the steps into the bar and joined them, Frank Kelly following. Kate said, 'Ah, here come two freebooters, from One Para. Dillon, this one is my brother George.'

But it was Kelly that Dillon bothered with. 'I wouldn't wear a shoulder holster if I were you, son. It's too difficult to dump your gun in a bad situation. It's better in your pocket, and don't say stuff you or I'll say stuff you.'

Kelly actually smiled, and Kate said, 'Sit at the next table, Frank, so you can hear.'

He smiled again at Dillon. 'Yes, ma'am, like a good dog I obey.'

Dillon laughed out loud. 'Well, this dog I like. Can he have a drink?'

'Not on duty,' Kelly said. 'And by the way, I'm from County Down, too, you Fenian bastard.'

'So we know where we are.' Dillon smiled. 'Go on, have one Bushmills, and sit down and hear what the lady wants.'

Her story was quite convincing. 'The thing is, Dillon, we, that is, Rashid Investments, are moving into Ulster in a big way because of the peace process, but we're experiencing roadblocks, if you know what I mean. Our developments would bring high employment, but we're being leaned on.'

'So?' Dillon asked.

'Well, we need what I suppose you would call protection. People who might help.'

'And who might that be?'

She waved to a waiter and paused until he'd poured more champagne. 'Have you heard of a man called Aidan Bell?'

Dillon almost fell over the table laughing. 'Jesus, girl, he's tried to shoot me more than once. Our Aidan was big with what you might call fringe organizations on the hard right of the IRA.'

'I heard he was possibly responsible for killing Lord Mountbatten.'

'Well, I was accused of that myself.'

'They also say you attacked Number Ten Downing

Street in February ninety-one with mortar bombs.'

'Never proved.' He smiled. 'Mind you, if we'd had a bit more time . . .'

'All right,' she said. 'So you're a bad boy, but I need to get to Aidan Bell to see if we can do a deal. Protection, call it what you want. He lives in a place called Drumcree in County Down.'

'I know it well, I'm from Down myself, but then you know that.'

'I'm supposed to meet him on Thursday. I'll take George.' She turned to Kelly. 'Can I count on you, too?'

'Of course, ma'am.'

Dillon said to him, 'Good man yourself,' and turned to her. 'And you're asking for me? I work for Ferguson.'

'So you'll tell him. This isn't an intelligence matter. I want back-up, that's all, and in that damn place you're the best. What's the matter, doesn't Ferguson ever let you work freelance?'

'I'll see what the good Brigadier thinks, and I'll let you know.'

At Ferguson's flat later that night, he gave the Brigadier a rundown of what had taken place.

Hannah Bernstein heard it all, too. When Dillon was finished, Ferguson thought about it, then turned to her.

'What do you think?'

'On the surface, it makes sense. The Rashid outfit is definitely into Ulster these days, but so are a lot of people. On the other hand, it's a good story. Too good.'

Ferguson turned to Dillon, who smiled and said, 'I always believed in women coppers. She's right.'

Ferguson nodded. 'There's a hidden agenda. See if you can find out what, Sean.'

'There you go, calling me Sean again.' Dillon smiled. 'Still and all, things are quiet. I'll take a look.'

'And keep in touch,' Ferguson told him.

The Rashid Gulfstream flew from RAF Northolt, a popular venue with executive jets that found problems with the congestion of Heathrow. Besides the two pilots, the other people on board were Kate, Dillon, George Rashid and Kelly. Dillon had arrived last, and once they were in flight, he opened the bar box and found a half bottle of Bushmills.

'We still don't know what's happening,' Kate said.

'Well, it's reasonably simple. Aidan Bell at Drumcree is expecting you sometime tomorrow to discover whatever you want to discuss with him. We land this afternoon at Aldergrove. My arrangements are that we go to a little fishing port called Magee, sail overnight to Drumcree and you can see Bell in the morning.'

There was silence. She said, 'Are you sure about this?'

'It's a nice forty-foot boat called *Aran*. I could handle it myself, but these two can act as deckhands. It leaves Aidan Bell slightly left-footed, you arriving that way – he won't expect it – so a bright girl should do rather well.'

'Bastard,' she told him. 'Why is it I think of you like that?'

'Because that's what I am.'

'Well, as long as you're my bastard on this thing, all right?'

Not that she believed him, not for a moment, but she had her agenda and she was playing it through.

The flight was normal, the drive down to the coast just as uneventful. Magee was a small place, the kind that in the old days had been mainly occupied with fishing. The *Aran* was tied up at the pier, a shabby boat, as Dillon had said, forty feet, but having used Ferguson's best efforts, he knew it had twin screws and the kind of engine you needed for action by night. He waited until almost midnight before leaving.

They had a simple meal of fried eggs and canned spaghetti bolognese, and even split a bottle of white wine so cheap that it had a screw cap instead of a cork.

'We'll take our leave,' Dillon said. 'The weather isn't too bad. Wind's six or seven. Half engines mostly.' He nodded to George and Kelly. 'You two cast off, then I suggest you get some sleep. There's no way of knowing how things will go in the morning.'

'And what about you?' Kate asked.

'I'll manage.'

'Dillon, I've been sailing boats for years.'

'Then if it gets rough, you can give me a hand.'

As the *Aran* moved out to sea, the tide was still running in. Visibility was poor, rain drifting. Kate stood beside Dillon in the wheelhouse, with only the light over the chart table.

'Rain squalls and maybe fog in the morning,' he

said. 'Are you okay? There are sea-sickness pills in that drawer.'

'I told you, Dillon, I've sailed before. I'll make some tea and perhaps a sandwich.'

Not long afterwards, he smelled bacon, and she came into the wheelhouse with a thermos flask of tea and three sandwiches.

'Two for you, one for me.'

'And you half Bedu, eating bacon.'

'Islam is a wonderful moral faith, Dillon.'

'And how does that sit with those twelfth-century Dauncey Christians?'

'Oh, they were hard people and their beliefs were very similar in some ways. You know something, Dillon? I'm half Bedu, but my God, I'm proud of my Dauncey roots. There are a lot of great ancestors there.'

Dillon finished his second bacon sandwich. 'It's an unusual situation, I can see that. I'm not sure about the aristocracy, Kate, but I like you. What about George and Kelly?'

'Last seen getting their heads down.'

'Good. I'll do the same, and since you keep boasting of your sailing prowess, I'll hand it over.'

When he returned four hours later, it was to a rolling motion. He had been lying on one of the bench seats in the saloon, come awake slowly and gone up the companionway. He opened the door of the wheelhouse to the sight of dawn, a grey light, heavy mist and rain, and the Down coast a couple of miles away. Kate stood there, hands steady on the wheel.

'Good man yourself,' Dillon said. 'I'll take over.' He eased her aside. 'Are you okay?'

'Fine. I haven't enjoyed anything so much in years. I'll make some tea. Would you like some more sandwiches?'

'See what the deckhands want. I'd say we'll arrive at Drumcree in about an hour. I know the place from the old days. There's a pub called the Royal George. Don't be misled by the name. It's a hotbed of Republicanism. We'll call in and ask for Bell.'

'Surprise him, is that your tactic?'

'Oh, you could say that. Let me be sure I've got this straight, Kate Rashid. You don't want me there when you meet him, am I right?'

'It's business, Dillon, private company business. George can come with me.'

'Fine,' Sean Dillon told her and turned the wheel. 'Now what about that tea?'

George and Kelly joined them eventually in the

wheelhouse, drank mugs of tea, and listened to Dillon.

'The pub, the Royal George, is a good Fenian institution and right on the jetty. You've both done Ulster time, so you know the kind of place.'

'Should we be carrying?' Kelly asked.

'Feel under the chart table. There's a catch.'

A flap fell down, Kelly pulled out a drawer and there was an assortment of handguns inside. 'I'll take the Walther in my pocket, so when I'm searched they'll discover it,' Dillon said. 'You'll find three ankle holsters with short-barrelled two-twos. One for each of us.'

'You think we'll need them?' George asked him.

'This is Indian territory and I'm one of the Indians.' Dillon smiled. 'Keep the faith, people. Slow and easy.'

Drumcree was a small place, with a tiny harbour, a jetty, a scattering of houses in grey stone and a few fishing boats. They coasted in, Dillon eased to the jetty, and George jumped over the rail and tied up. It was very quiet, no one about.

'There you go, Kate,' Dillon pointed. 'The Royal George.'

It was obviously eighteenth-century, but the roof looked sound and the sign was in green, with black lettering and what looked like fresh gilding.

'So what do we do?' Kate demanded.

'Well, like any decent pub in these parts, they'll do an Irish breakfast. I'd say let's partake and I'll tell mine host to inform Aidan Bell we're here.'

'And that will do it?'

'Absolutely. We're already on their screen, as they say.' He turned to the other two. 'You stay with the boat, Kelly, and be prepared for anything.'

A bell tinkled as they went in the bar. Dillon and George were in jerseys and reefer coats, Kate wore a black jumpsuit and carried a briefcase. There were three men sitting in the window seat eating breakfast; one was middle-aged with a beard, the other two were younger. They turned to stare, men of a rough persuasion with hard faces. A man appeared behind the bar, thickset, white-haired.

'Can I help you?'

'We'd like breakfast,' Kate said.

The well-bred English voice sliced through the quiet like a knife, and the men at the window continued to stare.

'Breakfast?' the man said.

Dillon cut in, making his Belfast accent even more pronounced. 'That's it, me ould son, three Ulster fry-ups. We've just sailed in from Magee. Then phone Aidan Bell and tell him Lady Kate Rashid is here.'

'Phone Aidan Bell?' the man said.

'What's your name?' Dillon asked.

'Patrick Murphy,' the man replied, as a reflex.

'Good man yourself, Patrick, now breakfast and Bell, in whatever order you want.'

Murphy hesitated and then said, 'Take a seat.'

Which they did, on the opposite side from the three men. Dillon lit a cigarette, there was a murmur of conversation, then the bearded man got up and crossed to the table. He stood there looking at them.

'English, is it?' he said to Kate, then leaned down and brushed her face. 'Still, I suppose anything's better than nothing where a woman's concerned. Come on, English bitch, let's see what you've got.'

There was a large bottle of brown sauce on the table. George tried to get up, but Dillon pushed him down, picked up the bottle and smashed it across the side of the man's head, sending him to his knees. The man knelt, blood and sauce on

his cheek, and Dillon stamped on his face, sending
him sprawling.

Patrick Murphy appeared at that moment and
was totally shocked as the two young men jumped
up and Dillon produced his Walther.

'I don't think so.'

'For Christ's sake,' the barman said. 'What are
you doing? They're Provisional IRA.'

'Once in, never out, I was told,' Dillon said.
'And I've been a member since I was nineteen.
I'll tell you what, Martin McGuinness wouldn't
approve of this lot. I mean, he's a family man.'
He turned to the two young men and nodded to
the floor. 'Get this piece of dung out of here.'

Their rage was plain, but they got the bearded
man to his feet. Behind them, the door swung open
and a man almost as small as Dillon strode in, dark
hair tousled, needing a shave, wearing a Barbour
jacket against the rain, with a large red-haired man
behind.

'Jesus,' he said. 'Is that you, Quinn, and in a
damn bad way?' He laughed out loud. 'And whose
toes did you stand on?'

'Mine,' Dillon said.

Bell turned in astonishment and his expression
was close to awe. 'Dear God, is it you?'

'As ever was. A long time ago it was: Derry, and those Brit paratroopers chasing us through the sewers.'

'You saved my life once.' Bell held out his hand.

'You tried to kill me twice.'

'Ah, well, so we had a falling out.' Bell turned to the two men supporting Quinn. 'Get him out of my sight.'

They took the bearded man out of the door and Bell said, 'What in the hell goes on, Dillon?'

'This is Lady Kate Rashid. I believe you have a meeting arranged.'

Bell didn't even look surprised. 'I should have known. Take me unawares, is that it? And where does this bastard fit in?' he asked her.

'Mr Dillon is acting in a private capacity. I wanted his expertise on County Down, and he's been provided with ten thousand pounds to supply it.'

'Flew into Aldergrove yesterday. Boated out overnight, back to Magee in an hour or two. Money for old rope,' Dillon said.

'Come off it, you still work for Ferguson, you turncoat.' He took a Browning from his pocket. 'Hands high. See to him, Liam.'

The red-haired man ran his hands over Dillon

and found the Walther. He turned to Kate. 'Now you, darling.'

It was Bell who said, 'Mind your manners, Casey, a lady this.' He gestured to the briefcase. 'See what's in there.'

'No, Mr Bell,' Kate told him. 'What's in there is between you and me.'

'I see.' He turned to George as Liam Casey checked him. 'This would be the younger brother? One Para.'

'You're well informed,' said Kate.

'I always am, and if your head of security is on that boat, he's also One Para and a damned Prod.'

'Which you are yourself,' Dillon reminded him and shrugged to Kate. 'One of the few in the IRA.'

'So what am I doing here?' Bell asked.

'Business, Mr Bell. As you're so well informed, you'll know I am Executive Chairman of Rashid Investments, and you'll know we have big plans for development in Ulster.'

'I had heard.'

'Can we talk?'

Bell nodded to the barman. 'We'll use the snug.' He led the way to a door, opened it to usher her through, and turned to Dillon. 'Sean?'

'You still don't understand,' Kate told him. 'Dillon is here only as a minder. My business is with you, and you alone, on behalf of Rashid Investments.' She turned and nodded to her brother. 'George, join us.'

The door closed. Dillon turned and said to the barman, 'I know it's early in the day, but it's cold out there and pouring with rain, and I'm County Down myself, so let's celebrate and get the Bushmills out.'

There was a fire in the open hearth of the snug, chairs on each side and a small coffee table in between. Kate Rashid sat down, her brother standing behind; Bell sat opposite and lit a cigarette, Liam Casey stood behind.

'So, the word is that Rashid Investments are having problems with their plans in Northern Ireland, and need a little protection.'

'Not really, Mr Bell. That's a story even Dillon believes. No, I don't need you to guard the door, as it were; you're far too talented for that.'

'Really? Then what do you need me for?'

'Last year you killed General Petrovsky in Chechnya, and also blew up most of his staff.

The world in general thought the Chechen freedom fighters had scored a great coup, but I know that you were paid one million pounds by Chechen sources in exile in Paris.'

'Do you now?'

'Oh, yes.'

His face was calm. 'You or your famous brother, the Earl, isn't it? A man to reckon with, and all the money in the world, I hear.'

'Not quite, but close. You've never met, of course.'

'Almost. He was a Lieutenant in the Grenadier Guards. Crossmaglen in South Armagh. I was with one of my best snipers. Your brother and a small patrol were moving in. My man had him in his sights, then a helicopter dropped in with another twenty Guardsmen and we had to run for it.'

'If you'd shot him, you'd have missed a big payday.' She pushed the briefcase across. 'Have a look.'

He flicked the catches and lifted the lid. Inside were rows of fifty-pound notes. 'How much?' he asked.

'A hundred thousand pounds as evidence of good faith. You keep it, whatever happens. My brother's gift to you.'

'And what do I have to do?'

'You may or may not know about this, but the Americans and Russians intend to prospect for oil in Hazar. The Sultan brokered a deal for them. It involved assassinating my brother.'

'The Sultan's dead. It was in the papers.'

'Exactly. One of his assassins almost killed me. My brother shot him dead. He's that kind of man.'

'He would be. Irish time, Lady Kate. Me, Dillon, Casey here, your brother – we're all cut from the same piece of cloth. But there's more here. I know I'm a bastard, but I'm a clever bastard.'

'All right. I'll tell you. It involves my mother and a man called Igor Gatov.'

Afterwards, Aidan Bell said, 'Excuse the language, but they're all fucks. The Americans, Russians, Brits. They use people, then throw them away like a paper cup.'

'So for once, we teach them a lesson. And I do mean a big lesson. We go straight to the top. I hear Jake Cazalet is a good man, but so what? Someone pays for people like Gatov, and ultimately it must be the one in supreme power. For President Jake Cazalet, you get two million. Now are you in or out?'

Liam Casey said, 'Jesus.'

Bell sat looking at her. 'You're mad, woman.'

'No, perfectly serious. As I said, you keep the hundred thousand, no matter what.' She took a phonecard from her purse, and a pen. She wrote quickly. 'My coded mobile number. You've got seven days. My brother and I will be at Trump Tower in New York next Thursday at our apartment. If you're interested, present yourself, plus a coherent plan. If not, you're one hundred thousand pounds richer and no hard feelings.'

Bell smiled. 'I'll be there, Lady Kate, Trump Tower, Thursday.'

She nodded, a certain satisfaction on her face. 'It was never the money, was it? It's the game to you, just like Dillon.'

'Well, I still expect to be paid, and for a job like this, I'll expect not two but three million sterling.'

He held out his hand and she took it. 'Somehow, I thought you'd say something like that.'

'We'll meet again next week then, in Manhattan.'

'I'll be there.'

Casey opened the door for her and they went out to Dillon, who was at the bar drinking Bushmills.

'A little early, even for you,' she told him.

'We have to walk back through the rain, girl. I like to keep the cold out. We're all done here, I presume?'

'Yes, back to Magee,' she said.

Dillon turned to Bell. 'A sincere sensation, Aidan. I'm sure you'll do whatever the lady wants with your usual ruthless efficiency.'

'Oh, you can count on it, Sean.'

Kate, Dillon and George went out, and Bell and Casey stood in the door and watched them go.

Casey said, 'It's madness, Aidan. Even you couldn't get away with it.'

Bell smiled, looking incredibly dangerous. 'Now that's where you're wrong, Liam. I can get away with anything. There's something burning in my brain already, something I read recently. I'll go and check it out. That's a hell of a woman.' He watched her go, Dillon and George on either side. 'But Dillon. That's a strange one, having him here.'

'A "minder", she said.'

'Could be, but he still works for Ferguson, which means he can't be in on this business. It wouldn't make sense.'

They walked out into the rain and moved towards the harbour at the same moment that Kate Rashid and the two men reached the *Aran* and stepped over the rail – and found Frank Kelly face-down on the deck. Quinn, the bearded man from the Royal George, came out of the wheelhouse with a savage grin, backed by his two cronies. They were all armed.

Without hesitation, Dillon flung himself over the rail into the harbour, dived deep and swam, surfacing at the stern.

Quinn was shouting, 'Get the bastard, get him!'

Dillon reached to the ankle holster and drew the .22 pistol. The men above looked over the rail and he shot each one between the eyes. Quinn, shocked, turned to see what was going on and George Rashid pulled the .22 from his own ankle holster and shot him in the right arm. Quinn dropped his gun, scrambled over the rail, and stumbled away.

George took careful aim just as Dillon came back up over the rail. 'Let him go and let's get out of here. See to Kelly,' he added to Kate, then moved to the wheelhouse and started the engines.

On the way down from the Royal George, Bell and Casey saw what was going on below on the boat.

Bell said, 'That shite Quinn. He's going to ruin

everything. Come on,' and he ran down the hill to the harbour.

They saw the action, Dillon taking to the water and shooting Quinn's two sidekicks, Quinn being shot by George Rashid and running for cover. Bell and Casey paused, watched George cast off and the *Aran* move out of the harbour, saw Quinn stumble between the boats on the beach.

'I've had it, Liam,' Bell said. 'The Provisional IRA can go to hell. This is my patch and this bastard has come close to screwing up the biggest job of my life. This time he goes down.'

He ran, followed by Casey. In working his way round the beach, Quinn had to wade through water, and when he turned around the stern of a fishing boat, he found Bell and Casey facing him.

'Aidan?' he said.

Bell smiled. 'You've been a stone in my shoe too long, you bastard. Let's end it now.' He drew a Browning from his pocket and double-tapped Quinn in the heart. Quinn fell back in the water, his body floating, half submerged.

Casey said, 'You want me to do anything?'

'No need, the tide's on the turn. It will take him out, and in Drumcree, who'll ask questions?'

*   *   *

The *Aran* moved out to sea. Kate went to the stern and sat in the rain using her coded mobile. Paul Rashid answered.

'It's me, darling.'

'How did it go?'

'I'll tell you when we meet. Bell will go for it.'

'Good. How was Dillon?'

'Well, he and Bell turned out to have shot at each other in the old days.'

'So, Dillon bought your story?'

'God knows. He's a devious bastard. What he did do was save my life.'

There was a pause and Paul Rashid said, 'Explain.'

Afterwards, he said, 'He doesn't take prisoners.'

'No. Mind you, George didn't let you down, either.'

'I'm proud of him. Tell him so for me. I'll see you soon.'

The *Aran* was plunging out to sea through strong waves. Dillon and George were in the wheelhouse, and Kate arrived with tea.

'How's Kelly?' Dillon asked.

'He'll be all right. A bash to the head, that's all. He'll have a headache for a while, but he's a tough nut.'

'Good,' Dillon said.

Dillon said, 'Now, Kate, there's half a bottle of Bushmills under the chart table.'

She found it, got it out, and poured into two mugs of tea. Dillon said, 'George, boy, as my Jewish friends would say, you're a *mensch*. My thanks.'

'Dillon, I've been through Sandhurst and One Para. Sometimes I forget the estate management.'

'Go on.' Dillon laughed. 'Get him out of here, Kate.'

When she was gone, he used her coded mobile phone to reach Ferguson. When the Brigadier answered, he gave him a rundown of events.

'Christ, Dillon, you've been killing again.'

'The ranks of the ungodly, Charles.'

'All right. Did you believe that story of hers, hiring Bell for protection for Rashid Investments?'

'Not for a moment.'

'So why involve you?'

'I've told you. I know Down and I knew Bell in the old days. I knocked off guys who wanted to knock her off. She hired me as a minder and mind her I did. Without me, she'd be dead.'

'And you still think there's something going on?'

'Absolutely. Something big, but I've no idea what.'

'Come home, Sean, and we'll think on it.'

At Aidan Bell's house, Casey was in the kitchen making tea. Suddenly the door opened and Bell appeared, a magazine in his hand.

'I was right, I found the story in *Time* magazine. It tells me exactly how to shoot Jake Cazalet.'

'You're mad,' Casey told him.

'Not at all, Liam. This could work. Trust me.'

MANHATTAN

———

LONDON

———

WEST SUSSEX

———

WHITE HOUSE

———

4

Aidan Bell and Liam Casey shared a suite at the Plaza Hotel beside New York's Central Park. They had flown over earlier on Concorde, the seats provided by Rashid Investments, and found a chauffeur-driven limousine waiting to take them to the hotel.

'This is the life, Aidan,' Casey said.

'Well, don't let it go to your head. Shave, shower and put your best suit on. It's like we're visiting royalty tonight. I don't want him to think we're straight out of the bogs.'

He showered in the second bathroom, then dressed in a white shirt, blue tie and an easy-fitting dark suit. When he went out to the sitting room, Liam Casey was standing at the window, looking out.

'Jesus, Aidan, what a town.'

He turned, wearing a black suit and shirt and black tie.

'Will I do?'

'You look like a bouncer at the Colosseum,' Bell said. 'Now let's go. We're only a couple of blocks away. Just behave yourself and do as I say, and this ought to go as smooth as butter.'

At Trump Tower, they went up in a private lift to the Rashid penthouse, where Kate opened the door. She wore a black dress and a gold chain round her neck, very understated.

'Mr Bell.'

'Lady Kate. What do I give to the woman who has everything?' He opened his briefcase and took out a cheap plastic box. 'A present from County Down. A sign of good luck. A four-leafed shamrock.'

'Well, we can do with lots of that, Mr Casey.' She nodded. 'In you come. My brothers are waiting.'

Paul Rashid sat by the fire in the drawing room with Michael and George. Kate made the introductions.

'Aidan Bell and his associate, Liam Casey.'

'Mr Bell.' Paul Rashid didn't shake hands. 'My sister tells me you almost had me shot in Crossmaglen.'

'True, but Allah was good to you,' Bell told him.

'I like that – I like it very much. You want a drink?'

'Perhaps later. For now, let's get to business, I think.'

'Fine. You wouldn't be here if you didn't think you could do it, am I right?'

Bell said, 'Yes, you are. Now, there are two common types of assassination. One is by nutcases who press through the crowd and shoot the President up close, with no chance of getting away. Often, they don't even *want* to get away. That's not for me. Two is the clever, complicated kind, the Day-of-the-Jackal thing, meticulously organized, every possibility accounted for – like I did in Chechnya when I got Petrovsky and his staff. That takes a long time to plan, however, and I sense you want results a little sooner.'

'You're quite right,' Paul said. 'So what's the answer?'

Bell smiled. 'There's a third way.'

There was silence. It was Kate who said, 'What, for God's sake?'

Bell was enjoying himself. 'Well, to shoot the President of the United States should be an impossibility – or could it be absurdly simple?' He opened his briefcase and took out a magazine. He held it up. 'America, like Britain, is a democracy. You can write anything you want about the great and the good. There's an article in here on Jake Cazalet, everyone's favourite President. It was in my head, so I looked it up, and it's all I need for a general plan. Now I only need to finish working out the details.'

The silence was profound. He smiled, feeling his power. 'I think I'd like a large Bushmills Irish whiskey and then we'll talk.'

A few minutes later, he stood on the terrace looking down at the traffic while Paul Rashid read the article, then passed it to the others.

'All right,' Paul said. 'Now, tell us your plan, Mr Bell.'

'As the article says, Jake Cazalet loves to spend his weekends at that old beach house on Nantucket. They helicopter him straight from the White House lawn to the house late Friday, and he spends Saturday and Sunday there before coming back Sunday night. He has no family, just that one daughter in Paris.

'Cazalet doesn't like a big fuss: he's notorious for it. At the house, even the cook and the housekeeper come in on a daily basis; they live in town. There are staff quarters, but he refuses to have more than two Secret Servicemen there at the weekend. I did a little extra research and learned that one is called Harper, he's the communications officer. The other is his favourite, a big, black, former Marine named Clancy Smith, who served in the Gulf War. Smith is devoted to Cazalet. He'd step in the way of the bullet if he had to. And then there's Blake Johnson.'

'Yes, the article mentions him. It says he is the Director of something called the General Affairs Department at the White House,' Rashid said.

'Known as the Basement, because that is where it is. In actuality, it's the President's private hit squad, totally separate from the CIA, the FBI or the Secret Service. It's been passed on from President to President for at least twenty years, no one knows quite how long. Johnson is also Cazalet's closest friend, a Vietnam vet with a strong record.'

'And you're sure of all this?' George Rashid said.

'I have to be. It's why I'm still alive.'

'Okay, so we've got a down-to-earth President who doesn't want a fuss and likes to be on his own,' said Paul. 'You know damn well that the perimeter of that area will be well monitored by the Secret Service.'

'Exactly.' Bell opened the briefcase again, took out a map and unfolded it. 'See, from the President's house we have a seafront of beach and sand dunes. But at the rear, we have this area of marsh, very unusual for Nantucket; it's the only spot like it on the island. It stretches in quite a way: high reeds, water, mud, a paradise for bird watchers. Cazalet loves it. Goes for a run along the paths every morning with his dog, and good old Clancy Smith running behind. Smith has a gun under his left arm and an earpiece, naturally, but there's no one else around, unless his friend Blake Johnson happens to be there that weekend and decides to join in the fun. If he turns up, I'll stiff him, too.'

There really was a heavy pause now and it was Kate who said, 'Everything you say makes sense, but there would be no way you would get inside the perimeter, inside the marsh.'

Bell smiled. 'Sorry, I haven't explained. You, my lord, have a house on Long Island, I believe?'

'That's right.'

'You'll supply me with a boat – a Sport Fisherman will do – and someone to pilot it. We'll sail up to the area and drift around a mile or so offshore. You'll also find me a Dolphin Speed

Trailer. Those things have two large batteries and travel underwater. Liam and I will go scuba diving, something we're good at, and then invade the marsh underwater into the reeds.'

'Then what?' Michael Rashid asked.

'Then wait for Cazalet, shoot him and Clancy Smith, and bugger off out of there. It'll take a little while for Harper to wonder why he hasn't heard anything and in that time we'll return with the Dolphin to the Sport Fisherman, then get back to Long Island, where you'll have a Gulfstream waiting to get us the hell out of there and onwards to Shannon.'

He paused, emptied his glass then said to Paul Rashid, 'Will it do?'

Rashid said calmly, 'I think it will do very well.' He turned to his brother George. 'Another Bushmills for Mr Bell.'

It was Kate who said, 'That's quite a script, but what if the script goes wrong? What if it doesn't work?'

'Nothing is certain in this life,' said Bell. 'There'll be dicey bits, but if we prepare this properly, it should work.'

'Then see that you do prepare properly,' said Paul. 'Remember, we'll only get one chance at this. If you fail, Cazalet's security will become so heightened it'll be impenetrable. And then we'll have to go through the trouble of finding another target.'

'Another target?' said Michael.

'I told you, brother. One way or another, *someone* is going to pay.'

There was silence. Then Bell turned to Kate. 'Will you be handling the organization of what we need?'

She glanced at Paul, then nodded. 'Anything you want.'

'All right. The Sport Fisherman I've already mentioned, the Dolphin Speed Trailer, diving equipment for two.'

'Weaponry?' Paul Rashid asked.

'I prefer basic AK assault rifles, with silencers. A couple of Brownings with Carswell silencers. That's all. Very simple, if things go well.'

'You said *if* again,' Kate told him.

Bell smiled. 'Oh, Lady Kate, I've been at it for twenty-eight years, and if you knew how often the best-laid schemes go wrong, you'd understand why I'm a cynic. Now' – Bell took a card from his pocket – 'your one hundred thousand pounds was nice, but I want the next instalment now. That's my Swiss bank account. One million on deposit against the three.'

Paul Rashid nodded. 'Of course.' He took the card and passed it to Michael. 'See to it.' He smiled. 'Champagne is indicated, I think.'

'A nice thought.' Bell smiled. 'But it's the last time. Once I start working, I stop drinking.'

'Well, that seems sensible.'

Kate offered champagne all round. Rashid raised his glass. 'So, we change the world.'

Bell laughed out loud. 'God bless, ould son, but if you believe that, you'll believe anything.'

Two days later, Kate Rashid took Bell and Casey down to the pier at Quogue, where they found a Sport Fisherman named *Alice Brown* and a man named Arthur Grant, who was fiftyish, with greying hair tied behind his neck.

'Mr Grant,' Kate said, 'these are the gentlemen I spoke about. They want a run up to Nantucket, to do a little diving. Mr Bell is looking for some interesting wrecks. You already have the Dolphin on board.'

Grant poured himself a Jack Daniel's. 'Well, lady, that's your story. Me, I think maybe they're up to something more than interesting wrecks, but I don't give a damn. Twenty thousand bucks, and she's yours.'

'Agreed.' She turned to Bell. 'Keep in touch,' and she went up the companionway.

Grant said, 'She's got a great ass on her.'

Bell dropped the bag containing the weaponry and kicked him on the right shin, then swung him around and Casey head-butted him. Grant fell back across onto the deck and Bell leaned over.

'From now on, you belong to me, Grant. Do we understand each other? Watch your mouth, do your job and you'll get the twenty grand. Otherwise –'

He nodded to Casey, who took a knife from his pocket, pressed a button and the blade jumped up.

'I'm sorry,' Grant said.

'Well, remember you're sorry,' Bell told him.

In London, Ferguson sat in his office at the Ministry of Defence working through papers. Detective Superintendent Hannah Bernstein came in.

'Anything for me?' Ferguson asked.

'Not much, sir. That business with the Rashids?'

'What?'

'Our information is they're all in New York. Some kind of family party.'

'What's Dillon up to?'

'Believe it or not, sir, he's gone shooting in West Sussex with Harry Salter. Pheasant.'

'Salter? That damn gangster?'

'Yes, sir, and young Billy.'

'The nephew? Wonderful. He's almost as bad as Harry.'

'I need hardly remind you, sir, he was a great help last time around on that job in Cornwall.'

'You don't need to remind me, Superintendent. But he's still a gangster.'

'He agreed to jump by parachute with no training whatsoever, and killed four of Jack Fox's men. Dillon would be dead without him.'

'Agreed. And he's still a damned gangster.'

At Compton House in West Sussex, it rained remorselessly, none of which bothered the shooting party. It was a syndicate of thirty that Harry Salter had paid into. He emerged from a long wheel-based Shogun wearing a cloth cap, a Barbour, jeans and rubber half-boots. He was sixty-five, with a fleshy and genial face until he stopped smiling. One of the most famous gang bosses in London, he'd been to prison only once in a long career.

These days he had millions in dockside developments and leisure construction, though the rackets being in his blood, he was still involved in smuggling from the Continent. There was a lot of money to be made from the cigarette trade. In Europe, they were incredibly cheap, but in Britain, the most expensive in the world. No need to get involved in drugs or prostitution when you had cigarette smuggling.

He stood in the rain. 'Bleeding marvellous. Isn't it bleeding marvellous, Dillon?'

'Country life, Harry.'

Dillon was wearing a cap and black bomber jacket. Billy Salter, Harry's nephew, a man in his late twenties with a pale face and wild eyes, emerged next, wearing cap and anorak. His uncle's right-hand man, he'd been in prison four times, all relatively short sentences for assault and grievous bodily harm.

'This is all your fault, Dillon. What have you got me into now?'

'Shoot a few pheasant, Billy, breathe the country

air. Last time out, it was villains trying to hit you. This should make a change.'

Joe Baxter and Sam Hall, Harry's two minders, dressed in jeans and anoraks.

'What a bunch of idiots.' Billy nodded at the other members of the syndicate emerging from Jeeps and Range Rovers.

'Why the funny gear? What are those ridiculous trousers?'

'It's how people like that dress to shoot, Billy,' Dillon said. 'It's an old English custom.'

The rest of the party was grouped around a large man with a florid face, and Dillon heard someone address him as Lord Portman. They all turned and looked at the Salter party with disfavour.

'Good God, what have we here?' Portman asked.

Another large man, this one with a grizzled beard, approached. 'Gentlemen, can I help? I'm the head keeper, Frobisher.'

'I should hope so, old son. Salter's the name – Harry Salter.'

Frobisher was astonished, hesitated, then turned to the others. 'This is Mr Harry Salter, president of the syndicate.' There were looks of horror.

Salter said, 'Lord Portman, is it?'

'That is correct,' Portman said frostily.

'Chairman of Riverside Construction, right? So we've got something in common.'

'I can't imagine what.'

'You don't have to imagine. I took you over last week. I'm Salter Enterprises, so, in a manner of speaking, you work for me.'

The horror on Portman's face was profound. He actually recoiled, and it was Dillon who said genially to Frobisher, 'Can we get on?'

Joe Baxter and Sam Hall were unloading the gun bags. Frobisher said, 'We'll space the valley up to that wood. I'll give you a number each.'

'We know how it works, old son,' Dillon told him. 'I've explained to my friends.'

Frobisher hesitated. 'So you have shot before?'

'Only people,' Billy told him. 'So let's get on with it.'

Three hours later, in the Shogun, Baxter was driving and Billy opened a bottle of champagne and poured it into plastic cups.

'What a bunch of toffee-nosed idiots. The look on their faces when I scooped the pool.'

'Yes, well, you have had a certain amount of practice,' Dillon said.

Harry Salter swallowed his champagne. 'That Portman's bleeding face was something to see.'

'Are you going to throw him out, Harry?' Billy asked.

'No, I know his track record and he's good. I'll improve his package. He'll come to heel. It's what's called business, Billy.'

'And bloody boring.' Billy turned to Dillon. 'You got anything on the go I could help with?'

'Back to Heidegger, is it, Billy? You feel the need for some action and passion?'

'Here, you lay off,' Salter told his nephew. 'Last time, we almost didn't get you back.'

'So, I'm bored,' Billy said. 'And you won't let me do the booze and cigarette runs from Amsterdam anymore.'

''Cos I don't want you nicked. Lesser mortals can take that chance. You just be a good boy.'

He poured more champagne, and Dillon said, 'I'll keep you in mind, Billy.'

Billy raised his glass. 'Always willing and available, Dillon.'

At the White House, Jake Cazalet sat at his desk in the Oval Office in shirtsleeves, working through a stack of paperwork. The door opened and Blake

Johnson came in. Outside, rain drove against the window. The President sat back.

'What have you got for me?'

'Hazar, Mr President.'

'The Sultan's death?'

'The Sultan's assassination.'

Jake Cazalet got up, went to the window, and looked out. Blake said, 'The CIA doesn't know anything about it, they say. They claim to be totally baffled. The question is: Baffled? Or embarrassed? We know the Sultan's people tried to kill Paul Rashid on behalf of our own oil interests and the Russians', and the Sultan was the CIA's man. I'd say they have a lot to answer for. And now, there's all this agitation from Hizbullah, Army of God, Sword of Allah, all the rest of them. Something's going on.'

'Dammit!' Jake Cazalet said. 'I don't like it at all.'

'It's a dirty world, Mr President. I can't prove it, but I'll lay you odds Rashid struck back.'

'Does Charles Ferguson know anything about it?'

'I don't know, Mr President. I haven't asked him.'

'Well, do so. Then get back to me.'

It was late in London as Ferguson sat by the fire of his flat in Cavendish Place and talked to Blake.

'I can't help you with the Sultan, although my personal feeling, too, is that it was a Rashid hit.'

'You're certain?'

'Absolutely. I have a trusted operative, Colonel Tony Villiers, commanding the Hazar Scouts as a contract officer. He keeps me well informed. During the Gulf War, he also commanded the SAS unit Rashid served in.'

'Well, that's close enough. Thanks, Charles. How's Dillon?'

Ferguson hesitated. 'Well, since you mentioned him . . . Dammit, Blake, this is strictly confidential, but . . . sit back, my friend, I've got a story to tell you. It concerns the Rashids.'

He went through everything: Drumcree, Aidan Bell, Kate Rashid, the shooting of the Provisional IRA men.

'My God,' Blake said. 'What are they up to?'

'So you don't believe their story either, do you? The Rashids *are* moving into Northern Ireland, that's a fact.'

'Maybe, but there's a lot more to all this than they're saying. Well, keep me informed, Charles.

Give my love to Hannah – and tell Dillon to watch his back.'

He put down the phone and went back to the Oval Office to bring the President up to date.

Nantucket

5

They made the trip from Long Island to Nantucket in the *Alice Brown* overnight. Arthur Grant took the wheel from Casey at midnight. Aidan Bell replaced him at four a.m.

It was still dark and the Irishman sat in the swivel seat, smoking a cigarette in the light of the binnacle, enjoying every minute of it and thinking about things.

He'd enjoyed seeing Dillon again, a great comrade in the old days, although their paths had altered, and he'd liked the girl. What a woman, and she'd seen right through him. It wasn't the money, never had been. He'd really showed those Russians in Chechnya: the General, with one round through his head at six hundred metres, and fifty pounds of Semtex for his staff. What they'd called an Ulster fry-up in the old days in the IRA . . . The door creaked open and Liam Casey came in with tea and sandwiches.

'I couldn't sleep. How are you?'

'Fine.' Aidan Bell put on the automatic pilot and took a sandwich as Casey poured tea into two mugs. 'How are you feeling?'

'I'll be fine myself, Aidan.'

'And why wouldn't you? We got away with it in Chechnya, didn't we?'

Casey took a sandwich himself. 'Yes, but the President of the United States, Aidan, that's something else again.'

'Ah, but what a ploy.'

He took another sandwich and Casey said, 'I've been thinking. What if Cazalet doesn't turn up this weekend? He must do that sometimes.'

'I checked his schedule, Liam. What am I, daft? I also checked CNN News earlier today on the TV there above the chart table. There was a mention of him going to the old family house by the sea as usual. This is America, they tell you everything.'

'Then why the hell didn't you tell me, Aidan?'

'Because Grant was in the wheelhouse at the time and you were on deck stowing the gear. What's it matter?'

Casey gave him a cigarette. 'I don't like him. He's what my old Gran used to call a sly boots.'

'Yes, well, if he crosses me, I'll cut off his boots

with his feet still inside, but don't worry. I've a story for him that should keep him happy. Leave it to me. Just make sure he doesn't get into the weaponry bag.'

It was raining slightly, more of a sea mist than anything else, as the *Alice Brown* drifted parallel to the coast three miles off Nantucket. Arthur Grant was at the wheel and Aidan Bell and Casey worked under the stern canopy, which they'd draped with fishing nets. They already had the Dolphin Speed Trailer over the rail and tied up and were checking their diving gear.

'Throttle back,' Bell called, and Grant did as he was told, so that they simply coasted along as Bell and Casey pulled on their diving suits and inflatables.

Grant had the windscreen open and leaned out. 'Any problems?'

'No,' Bell said. 'Put her on automatic and get down here.'

Bell eased on his jacket with the tanks attached and wrapped the Velcro straps, while Casey did the same.

Casey said, 'You're sure about this? Three miles in forty-five minutes?'

'It's easily done at the speed this thing goes. We'll

manage at fifteen feet all the way. We've plenty of air, and there's an onshore current.'

He dropped the weaponry bag over onto the Dolphin and clipped his holding line to his weight belt as Grant arrived. Bell pulled on his gloves.

'Well, it's the moment of truth. We're going on towards the coast looking for a World War II wreck. An Irish boat called *Rose of Tralee*.' The story was beginning to sound so good that he almost believed it himself. 'Amongst other things, it was carrying gold bullion from the Bank of England for safekeeping in Boston. People have been looking for her for years, but last month I traced an old guy of eighty-six who was a deckhand and survived when she was torpedoed by a U-boat. He didn't know about the gold, but he was able to give me the position.'

'Jesus Christ!' Grant said.

'So, play your cards right and I'll cut you in for a piece.'

'Sure. Anything you say, Mr Bell,' Grant said eagerly.

'Okay. You stay here. Drop your line. Get the nets out. Look busy. With luck, we'll see you in three hours.'

He pulled down his mask, put in his mouthpiece,

and went backwards over the stern rail. As he untied the line on the Dolphin, Casey joined him. Bell switched on the two heavy-duty batteries, mounted the front seating position and as Casey got on behind, took the Dolphin down, levelled off at fifteen feet and turned towards the distant coast of Nantucket Island with a surge of power.

Standing on the front porch of the old house, wearing a United States Marines tracksuit, Jake Cazalet drank his first cup of coffee of the day and watched Murchison, his beloved flatcoat retriever, walking with Clancy Smith on the beach below. There was a step behind, and as Cazalet turned, Blake Johnson joined him, also nursing a coffee.

'Always great to be back, Blake,' Cazalet told him.

'It sure is, Mr President.'

'Can't wait for my run. You'll join me?'

'If you'll excuse me, not this morning. Even though it's the weekend and early in the day, Harper is finding himself under considerable pressure in the Communications Room. There's a lot coming down from the Hill. I'd better stay and give him a hand.'

'All right, then come and look at my new toy. I had it shipped down during the week.'

He led the way round to the yard. The barn door stood open and inside was a large motorcycle on its stand. 'A Montesa dirt bike,' the President said. 'It'll be a lot of fun riding it along those roads.'

'I'll take your word for it,' Blake said. 'To be honest, Mr President, I haven't ridden a bike of any kind for years.'

'Hell, a child could work this thing. Shepherds use them to herd sheep.' He sat astride, started the engine, rode out and circled the yard. 'There you go.' He switched off and pushed it up on its stand. 'Feel free!'

'I will,' Blake said.

As they walked back to the porch, it started to rain. Murchison was sitting waiting, tongue hanging. Clancy Smith came over wearing a hooded oilskin coat in yellow and carrying another, which he passed to Cazalet.

'Knowing you, Mr President, I figure we're going, rain or no rain.'

'You're always so right, Clancy.' Cazalet pulled on the coat, buttoned it up, and whistled to Murchison. 'Come on, boy.'

He went down the steps and started to jog, the dog at his heels. Clancy Smith adjusted his earpiece, transferred his favourite old Browning from his shoulder holster to his right-hand pocket, and went after them.

Aidan Bell was not far off in his calculations and, helped by the strong current, they entered the estuary leading to the marsh in fifty minutes. It was a salt marsh, of course, a magnificent wilderness of tall reeds, deep water channels, mudflats, and birds of every description, who rose angrily as the Dolphin surfaced.

Bell coasted onto a sloping sandbank, then he and Casey dismounted, eased the Dolphin forward and got rid of their jackets and air bottles. All this was done in silence. Finally, Bell unclipped the weaponry bag, handed Casey an AK assault rifle and Browning, and took out his own. They stood there, strangely medieval in their black diving suits.

Bell said, 'One thing we know is that he always runs before breakfast. That could mean he's half-way round the roads already or that he'll turn up at any minute. But there's only one main road from the house leading to the marsh network. I'd say three or four hundred yards. We wait there – we're bound to get him either going in or coming out – so let's move in.'

He turned and led the way through the reeds, feeling cool, calm, and completely unemotional.

Jake Cazalet, Clancy and Murchison were running fast now in the heavy driving rain, and the President was enjoying every minute of it. As he had said more than once, it washed the years away, and with the world as it was, he could certainly do with that.

Murchison ran strongly at his heel, Clancy was five yards back, and he paused on an old plank bridge that was roofed over, a temporary shelter from the rain.

'You okay, Mr President?' Clancy asked.

'Fine. I'll have the usual.'

Clancy produced a packet of Marlboros, lit two and passed one to Cazalet, who took it and inhaled with deep pleasure.

'Don't let any press photographers see you doing that, Mr President.'

'Hell, I'm entitled to one weakness. These things

got me through Vietnam and you through the Gulf.'

'They surely did,' Clancy agreed.

They smoked in companionable silence, then ground out their cigarette butts. 'Let's go,' Cazalet said, and led the way out into the rain, breaking into a run again.

Hidden in the reeds beside the main road, Bell saw them coming. He whispered loudly across to Casey, who was on the other side.

'There they are. Get ready. You take the Secret Serviceman, I'll have the President, and don't be too eager. Take your time.'

He waited. There was no need for a long shot when it could be done virtually at point-blank range. He raised the AK to his shoulder, and Cazalet ran directly toward him.

And as Bell had told Kate Rashid, how often the best-laid schemes could go wrong. He'd planned meticulously, every contingency foreseen, except for the instincts of a flatcoat retriever named Murchison. With that special extra facility known only to dogs, he sensed something wrong, took off like a rocket and plunged into the reeds on the other side of the road.

Casey lurched out into the open, struggling to cope with the fact that Murchison had him by the left ankle, and his AK discharged.

Jake Cazalet stopped running some twenty-five yards away and Aidan Bell stayed hidden and took aim, but Clancy Smith was fast. In the same moment, he knocked the President sideways and took the bullet that Bell had intended for Cazalet in his right shoulder.

He staggered but never wavered. 'Take cover, Mr President,' he cried and shoved Cazalet down into the shelter of the reeds.

Cazalet gave a piercing whistle and, a moment later, Murchison joined them. There was blood in quantity pouring from the rent in Smith's yellow oilskin jacket.

'Is it bad?' Cazalet asked.

'I'll be all right. You'd better take this, Mr President,' and he passed the Browning across.

Bell called softly across the road, 'Stay out of sight, Liam,' and then he loosed off several bursts in the general direction where he'd seen Clancy Smith and Cazalet disappear.

Clancy was already calling in and Cazalet fired back twice.

In the Communications Room, Blake Johnson was seated next to Harper working through some signals when Clancy's voice crackled over the loudspeakers with the shocking words. 'Blake. Empire Down! Empire Down!' At the same moment came the sounds of gunfire.

Blake reached for the mike. 'Where are you?'

'Halfway along the main road. I've been hit, but the President is okay. He's doing the shooting back.'

'I'm on my way.' Blake turned to Harper. 'Give me your piece. You know what to do.'

Harper, face wild, handed him a Beretta. Blake slipped it into his right-hand pocket, ran straight out onto the porch and to the barn. A moment later, he rode out on the Montesa and hurtled along the road.

Peering through the reeds, Clancy and the President could see him coming when he was still some distance away. So, of course, could Bell and Liam.

'Crazy damn fool,' Cazalet said. 'He'll get himself killed. Why couldn't he wait till the cavalry got here?'

'That'll be the day,' Clancy Smith said.

Blake pushed the little bike up to sixty, a ludicrous speed on the narrow road, and Aidan Bell fired through the reeds, a short burst that exploded the front tyre and sent the Montesa into a long sliding skid on one side as Blake kicked free.

Liam Casey made a bad mistake then, and emerged from the reeds, AK raised.

'I've got you now, you bastard.'

Blake's hand came out of his right-hand pocket holding the Beretta, and he shot the big Irishman in the chest. Casey cried out, his AK discharging, and plunged headfirst into the reeds beside Bell.

Further along the road, Cazalet stood up briefly. 'Over here, Blake. I'll cover you.'

He dropped out of sight and Blake staggered along the road, limping.

Liam Casey said, 'Can you get the bastard who shot me, Aidan?'

Bell watched Blake go and disappear into the reeds. 'It's not worth it, Liam.'

'God, it hurts, Aidan.'

Bell took in the bullethole in the stomach of the diving suit. 'Yes, it would.'

In the far distance, there came an ominous rattling sound. 'Oh dear, here comes the heavy brigade. Time to go.'

'What do you mean?' Liam demanded.

'What I mean is you win some and you lose some, and this one is very definitely down the plughole, thanks to that damn dog. Cazalet will buy him a gold collar after this. I'll just keep their heads down over there and be on my way.'

He sprayed the reeds in the general direction of the President's party, emptying his AK, dropped it into the mud, and picked up Casey's.

'But what about me?' Casey moaned.

'That's a problem, but I have a solution. Our friends didn't see two of us, only one. So, if they find one, that should keep them happy while the other one gets away.'

He stood up and took his Browning with the Carswell silencer from inside his diving jacket. Liam Casey said, 'You can't leave me, Aidan.'

'I'm being practical.'

Aidan Bell aimed for a heart shot, the Browning coughed once, Liam Casey jerked and lay still.

'Sorry, old son,' Aidan said softly, then he put the Browning back inside his jacket and slipped off through the reeds. Four hundred yards away, the Dolphin waited; that wasn't too far, and then he'd be back underwater before the security helicopters started to blanket the area. On the other hand, they'd find Liam soon enough, and that should hold them.

After that long final burst, there was silence. 'Maybe he's down,' Cazalet said.

'Or out of it,' Clancy observed.

Murchison whined, then snuffled, nose up. 'Something's getting to him,' the President said.

The helicopters were close now, two of them. 'He won't wait around for this lot,' Blake said. 'He's either on his back or on his way. I'm going out.'

He stepped out of the reeds before the President could order otherwise and stood on the path and waved with both arms as the two Hawk helicopters swung down. They made their landings, each one disgorging six Secret Servicemen in navy-blue assault gear, each one carrying the new Parker-Hale machine pistol. They crowded round, and the President emerged, helping Clancy Smith, who had lost a considerable amount of blood.

'The President's fine,' Blake said.

'Only because Clancy took a bullet meant for me,' Cazalet said. 'Two of you get him into one of the choppers.'

'And you, Mr President, you know the rules. We take you straight out of harm's way till everything is sorted out,' Blake said.

'All right, damn you.' Cazalet whistled to Murchison and followed them as they took Clancy Smith.

One of the Hawks lifted off and Blake turned to the others. 'There was one man wearing a black diving suit. He tried to shoot me with an AK. I shot him for sure and he sort of dived into the reeds on that side down there. Don't come back without him.'

About the same time, Aidan Bell, back in his diving gear, was sliding the Dolphin into the water. He switched on, climbed on board and took her down to twenty feet as a precaution. Within ten minutes, he was moving out to sea.

'Always the great survivor, Aidan,' he told himself. 'Always the great survivor.'

They found Liam Casey and at first thought he was dead. One of them went for Blake, but by the time he'd arrived the situation had changed, and they were carrying him out of the reeds toward the second Hawk.

Campbell, the agent in charge, said, 'He's got a real bad stomach wound – your shot, I'd say, but you did say you only fired once.'

'Absolutely.'

'Then there's been someone else around. Someone tried a heart shot, probably to finish him off, but he had a Browning inside his jacket and it turned the bullet. I think he's on the way out, mind you.'

'Well, let's get him into surgery as soon as possible.' There was a military hospital on a small air force base twenty miles away on the main coast.

'I just heard the President's there already with Clancy,' Campbell told him.

'Then let's get moving.'

On the Hawk, they put Liam Casey on a stretcher, battle packs taped to his wounds. His eyes opened and he stared around him, and there was a kind of recognition when he saw Blake.

'I know you,' he whispered.

Blake leaned close. 'How do you know me?'

'The Basement. You're Dillon's friend. The Basement man.'

Blake had never been so astonished. 'How in the hell do you know that?' But there was no reply, for Liam Casey had passed out.

At the hospital, he was taken away and Blake found the President having coffee in a private lounge.

'How's Clancy, Mr President?' Blake asked.

'He'll be fine. He should get a medal. Hell, he shoved me aside and took that bullet, Blake. I've been informed you've found the assassin. How is he?'

'Being rushed into surgery. He spoke once.' Blake told him what the Irishman had said.

'The Basement man? Dillon's friend? Blake, what have we got here?'

'God knows, sir. We'll have to wait.'

'Well, one thing is certain. I don't want any publicity. Keep this totally under wraps. It never happened. You, me and the Secret Service – that's all who know. But what I want to know is: who is behind this, and why?'

'Should I call Ferguson, Mr President? The man did mention Dillon. I should check.'

'That makes sense. Okay, talk to Charles and Dillon, too. No one else.'

'Not Murchison, he already knows.'

Murchison, lying by the electric fire, got up and the President of the United States kissed him on the nose. 'He went straight for that bastard. Saved my life.'

'He's special, all right.' Blake smiled. 'Excuse me. I'll get on with this if you'll follow me, Mr President.'

The *Alice Brown* rose and fell on a heavy rolling swell as Bell surfaced on the Dolphin. Nets trailed into the water, all very businesslike, and Grant came to the stern rail.

Bell undid the Velcro ties of his jacket and eased off his air bottles into the water. He pulled off his mask and flippers; the AK he had dropped off a mile back.

'Throw me a line.'

Grant frowned. 'Where's your friend?'

'There was an accident.'

Grant didn't like it, his face clouding. 'Now look, what's going on here?'

Bell unzipped his nylon diving jacket, produced the Browning, and shot him between the eyes. Then he reached for the rail and pulled himself over and turned and fired several shots into the Dolphin, which started to settle into the water. He went through the lockers in the wheelhouse and found a length of chain, which he wound around Grant's ankles before pushing him under the rail. The body slid under the surface and Bell hauled in the nets quickly, then went below, got a bottle of Irish from the galley and hurried back on deck. He went into the wheelhouse, switched on the engines and moved away, one hand on the wheel while he poured whiskey, a very large one, into a plastic cup. He swallowed the lot, then poured another as rain started again.

In the living room of the great house at Quogue, Paul and Kate Rashid sat by a log fire. Michael and George were in London. Rashid's coded mobile rang, he answered and found Bell.

'What news?'

'There was a screw-up. This is the story.'

He gave an account of what had happened, which was a reasonably true version, omitting only the fact that he'd finished off Liam Casey.

'I'd like to say I'm sorry,' Bell said, 'but I did nothing wrong and everything right. It was just that damned dog.'

'You know what the Arabs say? *Inshallah*. As God wills,' Paul Rashid told him. 'You couldn't shoot the dog?'

'There was no time.'

'When will you arrive?'

'Four hours.'

'All right. I'll have the Gulfstream waiting at Westhampton Airport. My sister is here. We'll fly back to the UK together.'

'Suits me.'

'What about Grant? I hate loose ends.'

'Taken care of. What's the expression? Arthur Grant is asleep with the fishes.'

'And what about his boat?'

'I'll swim ashore.'

'We'll see you soon, then.'

Paul Rashid switched off and turned to Kate. 'A dog – a flatcoat retriever called Murchison.' He started to laugh, then he reached for his mobile. 'I'll phone the airport and tell them to get the Gulfstream ready. Then we'll have a glass of champagne.'

'But what do we drink to?'

'Why, Murchison, of course.'

At the hospital, the fight for Clancy Smith's life continued for four hours. The Air Force flew in two additional trauma surgeons and the President's own doctor.

After the surgery, Cazalet and Blake sat for a while with Clancy, whose pain had been dulled by drugs. The chief surgeon came in and had a look at him.

'You'll be fine, son, just fine.'

'Thank you, sir.'

The surgeon nodded to Cazalet, who followed him out. 'Mr President, does this mean what I think it means?'

'Robert, I need your holy oath on this,' Cazalet said.

'Of course, Mr President. That was an AK bullet we took out of that young man. I had one in me myself in Vietnam.'

'Well, this one was meant for me, and that brave boy pushed me aside, turned his back and took it for me.'

'God in heaven. And the other?'

'Is the assassin, although we think there could have been another one, too. Will he live?'

'Debatable. I'll keep you posted. We're just finishing in there.'

Cazalet went back in the room and brought Blake up to date. 'Let's hope he survives. It's a bizarre business and I'd like an answer.'

Clancy was drifting off. 'Do I still have a job, Mr President, or are you having Campbell move someone else in?'

'Over my dead body.'

Clancy started to laugh helplessly. 'God, that hurts, but you've got to admit it's kind of funny.'

'Get some sleep, Clancy,' Blake said. 'The President and I are going to grab something to eat. We'll see you later.'

Aidan Bell was really lucky on the final approach to Quogue in the *Alice Brown*. There was a heavy sea mist blanketing everything. He tipped the dinghy over the side with its small outboard about

half a mile out, then went below and opened the
seacocks. He went over the side, switched on the
outboard and moved some little distance away
and waited. It didn't take long. The *Alice Brown*
settled, decks awash, then went very quickly. Bell
opened the throttle and sped away toward the
shore.

In the living room, Rashid and his sister were
talking. 'So what now?' she asked.

'I have an alternative target. I always did.'

'Am I permitted to know?'

'Soon, my dear, but not yet.'

There was a rapping at the french windows. Paul
Rashid opened a drawer near at hand and took out
a Walther. He stood up and nodded to Kate. It
was Bell standing out there. When she opened the
window, he stepped in with a smile, still wearing
the diving suit.

'God bless all here, that's what the Fenians say.'

'You're all right?' she asked.

'Yes. Just show me where you parked my bags. A
shower and a change of clothes and I'm ready.'

'Then make it fast,' Paul Rashid said. 'We're
leaving Westhampton in one hour.'

'Has there been any news on the television yet?'

'There hasn't been a hint, which I find very strange. I don't like it, so let's get moving.'

At the hospital, the President slept on a small bed in one of the interns' rooms. Blake dozed in a chair in the lounge and came awake to a hand on his shoulder. He looked up and found one of the surgeons, an Air Force Colonel, there.

'Mr Johnson. He's come round, but it's not good. He's very weak.'

'Can I talk to him?'

'You can try, but I don't think you'll get much.'

'Fine. Notify the President. I'll go in.'

Liam Casey lay there, wired up to life support. A male nurse was in attendance.

'I've got permission to try and speak to him,' Blake said.

'I don't think you'll get far, sir.'

Blake pulled a chair forward and Casey opened his eyes. For a little while, his voice proved surprisingly strong.

'I'm dying, aren't I, and you're the guy who shot me. The Basement man. Dillon's friend.'

'Look, what do I call you?'

Behind him, the President and the Colonel eased into the room.

'I don't suppose it makes any difference now. Casey – Liam Casey.'

'Where are you from?'

There was a little blood on Casey's mouth and the nurse wiped it away.

'Drumcree. County Down.'

Blake frowned. 'I've heard of Drumcree, but why do you call me the Basement Man, Dillon's friend?'

''Cos I've seen your details in the file, your picture.'

'Which file?'

'The file Aidan prepared, the plan to do away with the President. Three million she promised when she saw us in Drumcree. She lied to Dillon, told him she was looking for protection for some business enterprise in Northern Ireland.'

The President said, 'What in the hell is going on?'

Blake waved him down and said to Liam, 'So Aidan is Aidan Bell and he was here and tried to shoot the President?'

'Shot me. I thought he'd finished me off. Left me to carry the can and cleared off.'

'How?'

'Underwater.' He seemed suddenly stronger. 'Fishing boat three miles out, then back to Long Island. They have a house. The Rashids have a house.'

'Just take it easy.' Blake soothed him. 'Why? Why would Paul Rashid want the President dead?'

'American Russian double agent called Gatov killed his mother, so he killed him. The Arabs tried to kill Rashid for some Yank and Russian oil people. He wanted revenge.'

'Only he didn't get it, did he? He failed?'

'That's all right. Alternative target.'

'What would that be?'

'Rashid said it would be his choice.'

Suddenly, he grimaced in pain and moved convulsively. The male nurse and the Colonel went in fast and Blake got out of the way.

'Please leave, gentlemen,' the Colonel asked.

In the lounge, the President said, 'For God's sake, what goes on?'

'Let me remind you, Mr President, of my conversation with Charles Ferguson not too long ago, concerning a trip Lady Kate Rashid made to County Down using Sean Dillon as her minder.'

*   *   *

118

When Blake went into the lounge a little while later, the President was drinking coffee, a frown on his face. He looked up. 'Well?'

'Casey's dead. I've spoken to Harper in the Communications Room. He's checking out the Long Island situation, the Rashids.'

Cazalet lit a Marlboro, got up, and paced around. 'It beggars belief. Rashid is one of the richest men in the world, an earl, a war hero, a friend of royalty. Who in the hell would believe it?'

'Nobody, Mr President, nobody in the wide world. Casey's dead, and what he said could easily be dismissed as the ramblings of a dying man. Right now, we've got nothing to use against Rashid.'

'But why is he so determined, Blake?' Cazalet asked.

'A lot of reasons, I suspect. The attempt on his own life, the death of his mother, the perfidy of the Sultan, his desire to rid Hazar of our influence. We're the Great Satan, don't forget that. He may be English, but that Bedu side – well, I wouldn't like to be alone with him in the desert.'

Cazalet said, 'All that money. It means nothing to him, does it?'

'It's just a tool of power. It lets him fly down there in a helicopter so that he can roam on a camel with his warriors. There's nothing more important to him.'

There was a long pause. Cazalet was about to speak when Blake's mobile rang. He answered, listened, then said, 'Fine, I'll get back to you.'

'Harper. The Rashids were in Quogue.'

'And?'

'Flew out of Westhampton four hours ago. Paul and Kate Rashid, and some man named Thomas Anderson.'

'Aidan Bell?'

'I'd say so. Destination Northolt RAF base.'

There was a long pause before Cazalet said, 'There's nothing we can do, is there?'

'To be frank, no, not at the moment. But I'll speak to Ferguson.'

'Right. Do that, then get to London yourself. I want you to coordinate everything with the Brigadier.'

'Actually, he's just been promoted. Major General now.'

'Really? I'm very glad. I'll speak to him myself before you leave, but for the moment, it's been a hell of a day, so let's get back to the house.'

*   *   *

On the Gulfstream, halfway across the Atlantic, the Rashids and Bell had a light meal of smoked salmon, salad and champagne.

Bell emptied his glass. 'So what next?'

'I'm thinking about it,' Paul Rashid told him. 'I've other problems in Hazar. I'll be in touch.'

'Well, don't leave it too long. In the meantime, I'll go back to Drumcree and check that things are in order, that the lads are behaving themselves.'

'I'm sure they are,' Kate Rashid said.

'They usually do. They don't like to upset me.'

Aidan Bell tipped his chair back and closed his eyes. It had, after all, been a long day.

LONDON

6

At Cavendish Place, late that night, Ferguson sat with Dillon and Hannah Bernstein and went over the whole business. After hashing it out for hours, with no particular conclusion, Ferguson said, 'All right, so his personal hit man, this Aidan Bell, failed with Cazalet by a stroke of good fortune. I don't think they'll try him again now. So who's the alternative target?'

Hannah Bernstein said, 'As he seems to have it in for both the Americans and Russians, General, what about the Russian premier?'

'I can't see even Aidan Bell operating in Moscow,' Dillon observed.

'He wouldn't have to,' Ferguson said gloomily. 'The Premier is due in London on the seventeenth of next month. Trade talks with the Prime Minister.'

'I didn't know that, sir,' Hannah said.

'It isn't public knowledge, Superintendent. But that's only six weeks away.'

'So you think he could be the target?'

'How do I know? What do you think, Dillon?'

'It's a bit obvious.'

'So's Cazalet, if you think about it in hindsight. A wonderful thing, hindsight. Who else could it be?'

'Beats me,' Dillon said. 'So the best thing to do – is ask him.'

There was a stunned silence. Hannah Bernstein said, 'Ask him?'

Dillon turned to Ferguson. 'Brigadier . . .' He laughed. 'Sorry . . . General. In the past, you have talked about situations where they know that we know and we know that they know.'

'True.'

'So let's push the good Earl a little. Make sure he knows we know and that we're on his case.'

Ferguson nodded. 'Not a bad idea. Maybe it'll shake something loose, make him a little incautious. Let's wait until Blake arrives in the morning, then we'll beard Rashid in his den, as it were.'

'Excellent,' Dillon said. 'And Aidan is back, we assume, in Drumcree. Let's make sure. Can you get people to check on that, Charles? Aidan Bell may be minus Liam Casey, but he's still got Tommy Brosnan, Jack O'Hara, Pat Costello – a whole crew of blackguards. Let's make sure they're all still in County Down.'

The following evening, the Rashids walked into the Piano Bar at the Dorchester to find Sean Dillon seated at the piano. He was wearing a dark blue suit and a Guards tie, and a cigarette drooped from the corner of his mouth, unlit.

Kate Rashid walked over to him, flicked her gold lighter and lit his cigarette. 'Is that better?'

'God bless you, ma'am, for the decent soul you are, and I'll forgive you, only because I love you dearly, for conning me over our Drumcree trip.'

'Conning you?'

'Absolutely. I know all about the good Aidan trying to stiff the President. Very naughty, Kate, very naughty indeed.'

She lit her own cigarette. 'Why, Dillon, I never knew you for a fantasist.'

'Oh, I'm a realist all the way, sweetness. Aidan Bell tried to finish off Liam Casey on Nantucket, only Casey had a Browning tucked inside his diving jacket and it turned the bullet. Of course, that still left him with a bullet in the belly.'

'How interesting.'

'Still, he lived long enough to spill the beans. He was very annoyed with Aidan, Liam was.'

'Yes, well, he would be, I imagine,' Kate said.

'General Ferguson's due any minute, with Blake Johnson. I'd tell you who Blake is, but I'm sure you already know, don't you, Kate? I'd listen to what they have to say if I were you.'

She turned and went back to her brothers. They had their heads together for a while when Charles Ferguson appeared at the head of the stairs by the bar, with Hannah and Blake Johnson. They came down and joined the Rashids. As they sat, Dillon eased off the piano bench and went to join the others.

'So, Mr Dillon,' Paul Rashid said. 'What an extraordinary tale you have told my sister.'

'The eyewitness account is even better,' Blake told him. 'I was there. Liam Casey tried to shoot me and I was the one who shot him in the stomach. The wound killed him eventually, but we had a fine old chat, did Liam and me.'

'You can't prove any of this, you know,' Paul Rashid said.

'You're right,' Charles Ferguson told him. 'Not yet. But we intend to, Rashid. I intend to pursue you to the ends of the earth. Dillon here is particularly looking forward to it.'

'Is that so?' Paul Rashid smiled. 'It would appear you are declaring war on me, General Ferguson.'

'Exactly.'

Rashid stood up, followed by his two brothers and sister. 'Beware. I could declare *jihad* on you myself. But I do not think that will be necessary. Will it, General?'

He walked out, the others followed. Blake said, 'You really pushed him, Charles.'

Ferguson said, 'I intended to.' He looked at Hannah. 'What did you think?'

'You didn't leave him much room to manoeuvre.'

He turned to Dillon. 'And you?'

'Me?' Dillon laughed. 'Jesus, your honour. I'm just a simple Irish boy. What intrigued me was the fact that he didn't actually deny any of it.'

'Well, he's your business now,' Ferguson told Dillon. 'Stay on his case.'

Hannah said, 'We should remember what he said, sir. He really could declare war on us.'

'Are you querying my orders, Superintendent?'

Dillon said, 'Oh, don't worry. She's good at

taking orders, General, however stupid they are. I'm the one who looks at things differently, but then, as we both know, I've always been a little mad. Come on, Hannah, let's go and put the world to rights,' and he turned and led the way out, leaving Blake with Ferguson.

At Kate Rashid's house, Paul held a council of war with the other three.

'It's damn unfortunate Casey survived.'

'Even more unfortunate that Aidan Bell was economical with the truth,' Kate told him.

'True, but it's only to be expected with people like him. I'm going to let it go for now. I still need him.'

'So what happens now?'

'I think I'll teach Ferguson a lesson. He made Dillon into a direct threat, so it's time to get rid of Dillon.' He turned to Michael. 'That's your task. Use Ali Salim, from the Party of God. He's good enough. Only, keep out of it yourself.'

'And when do you want this business handled, brother?'

'As soon as possible. If Salim is available, let him get on with it now. But leave it up to him. You're a good boy, Michael, but not against the Dillons of this world.' He turned to Kate. 'You agree?'

'Absolutely.' She kissed Michael on the cheek. 'Just give it to Ali Salim.'

Dillon and Hannah had a light meal at a small Italian restaurant near his townhouse in Stable Mews. They'd discussed the situation until it was coming out of their ears, their chief worry being whether Ferguson had pushed it too hard or not. They were on tea and coffee when Blake, who had phoned on Dillon's mobile earlier, came in.

'You want something to eat?' Dillon asked.

'I had scrambled eggs with Ferguson at his place.' He sat down. 'I've spoken to the President. He thinks Paul Rashid is nuts.'

'Then if he is, so am I.' Dillon shook his head. 'The curse of our civilization these days has been the unrestricted growth of capitalism and the interference of Western companies into places like Arabia, intent only on making a buck. We're from societies that think money is everything. What we should realize is we can be dealing with people who think it means nothing, and the Bedu are like that.'

'That's all right for Rashid,' Blake said. 'He is a pretty rich Bedu.'

'Yes, but everything he's involved in is Bedu-controlled, Rashid-controlled. There's a difference. Anyway, do you want to walk round to my place, have a drink there?'

'I'm parked outside, we can drive,' Blake said.

He went out with Hannah, Dillon hung on to pay the bill, then went after them.

Ali Salim was a Yemeni Arab of thirty-five with wild eyes and a dark, pockmarked skin. He had accepted the contract without hesitation and made light of Dillon's reputation.

'So, this one is trouble, you say? I will give him more trouble than he has ever known. Where will I find him?'

They were in the sitting room of Ali's flat near Marble Arch. He opened a drawer and took out a Beretta. Michael was confused and unhappy. He found the man disturbing, but then his brother had been insistent that he stay out of the affair personally.

'He lives in Stable Mews, number five. I'll take you there in my car and drop you off.'

'Then let's do it.' Ali took a bunch of keys from a drawer. 'Picklocks, just in case he's not there to answer the door. Keep your money. This I do for your beloved brother, who is an example to us all.'

Dillon unlocked the front door and led the way in, Hannah following, Blake behind. They moved down the hall and entered the sitting room, and Ali Salim was there, standing behind the door. He struck Dillon a heavy blow across the side of the head with his Beretta. Dillon staggered across the room and fell to one knee.

Ali grabbed Hannah and pushed her hard, putting her on her knees, her purse flying from her hand. Salim pivoted and struck Blake a glancing blow across the head as well, then aimed his pistol at Dillon. Hannah grabbed for her purse, reached inside and took out her Walther and, glimpsing her out of the corner of his eye, Ali Salim turned and shot her three times.

Blake grabbed at Ali Salim's legs and was hit across the head again. Dillon got to his feet and reached inside the chimney to where he kept his ace in the hole, a Walther suspended from a nail by the trigger guard.

His hand swung up and he shot Ali Salim between the eyes, hurling him back over a chair. Ali writhed on the ground, blood all over his face, and Dillon stepped close and shot him twice in the heart.

He dropped to one knee and checked Hannah. Her eyes were glazed and there was blood everywhere. He got up, went to the phone and dialled.

'Rosedene? Dillon. There's been a major incident. Superintendent Bernstein's been shot three times. We're at my house. Get over here right away.'

He went into his bedroom, ransacked a cupboard and returned with two or three field service wound packs. 'Get these on her, Blake,' he said – Johnson was on his feet, looking no worse for wear – and went to Ali's body, searched it and came up with a wallet.

He phoned Ferguson. When the General answered, he said, 'I came back to my house with Hannah and Blake, and an Arab hit man was waiting. According to his ID, he's one Ali Salim. He shot Hannah three times, and I shot him dead. I've spoken to Rosedene. An ambulance is on the way.'

'Dear God,' Ferguson said.

'If I were you, I'd notify her family. I'll send Blake with her. I'll stay here to clean up.'

'Leave it to me,' Ferguson said, managing to stay calm.

Dillon used the phone again. There was an instant reply. 'Dillon here, I've got a disposal for you. Immediate. The consignment is at my place.'

'On our way,' a voice said.

Dillon replaced the receiver, the doorbell rang, and when he answered, three paramedics came in with a stretcher. He led the way into the sitting room, where Blake crouched by Hannah.

'Three gunshot wounds. Close range. This Beretta was used.' He handed over Ali Salim's weapon.

They busied themselves over her quickly, put her on a drip, then got her onto a stretcher.

'Go with her, Blake. I'll catch up.'

Suddenly he was alone. He lit a cigarette and went and poured a Bushmills. He drank it down and poured another, his hand shaking a little.

'If she dies, Rashid,' he said softly, 'then God help you.'

A moment later, the doorbell rang again. He answered and admitted two cadaverous middle-aged men in dark suits and overcoats, one of them with a bodybag in black plastic over his left arm.

'In here.'

Dillon led the way through. 'Dear me,' the older one said when he saw Ali Salim.

'Save your sympathy. He shot Superintendent Bernstein three times. I've got his wallet. I'll pass it on to General Ferguson. Just get him out of here.'

'Of course, Mr Dillon.'

Later, thinking about Hannah Bernstein and all they'd been through together, he felt not rage but concern. It was, after all, the business they were in. Rage would come later. He found a leather trenchcoat and let himself out.

Many people thought that Arnold Bernstein was the finest general surgeon in London, but to operate on his own daughter would have been unethical, which was why Professor Henry Bellamy of Guy's Hospital was in charge. He allowed Bernstein to observe in the operating theatre, which was as far as ethics would go.

Ferguson, Dillon, and Blake waited in the ante-room with Rabbi Julian Bernstein, Hannah's grand-father. They drank coffee and tea and waited through the four-hour operation.

'You must hate us all, Rabbi,' Ferguson told him.

The old man shrugged. 'How could I? This was the life she chose.'

The door opened, and Bellamy and Bernstein came out, still in their surgical gowns. They stood up and Ferguson said, 'How bad is it?'

'Very bad,' Bellamy told him. 'The stomach is damaged, the bladder, the spleen. One bullet went through the left lung, her spine is chipped. It's a miracle she's here.'

'But she is?' Dillon said.

'Yes, Sean, she is, and I think she'll pull through, but it's going to take time.'

'Thank God,' Rabbi Bernstein said.

'No, thank a great surgeon,' Dillon said, turned, and went out.

Ferguson called to him, 'Sean, wait.'

He caught up with Dillon on the front steps, Blake at his shoulder. 'Sean, you're not going to do anything stupid?'

'Now why would I do a thing like that?'

'I'll deal with Rashid.'

Dillon stood stone still, gazing at him. 'Then soon, General, soon. If you don't, I will. Just remember that.' And he went down the steps and walked away.

Blake Johnson said, 'An angry man, General.'

'Yes, and with every right to be. Let's talk things over, Blake, and see if we can come up with the right way to handle this.'

Back in Stable Mews, Dillon answered the door and found the older of the two men who had taken Ali Salim's body away. He was carrying a light black plastic urn.

'Ah, Mr Dillon. I presumed you'd want them.'

'What is it?'

'Ali Salim's ashes.'

Dillon took the urn. 'Excellent. I'll see they reach the right destination.'

He put the ashes on the hall stand, then phoned Ferguson. 'It's me. When are we seeing Rashid?'

'I'm not sure.'

'Well, I am. I told you: if you don't make a move, I'll face him myself.'

'There's no need for that. I'll phone him and arrange a meeting.'

'Do that.' Dillon put the phone down.

To his surprise, the doorbell sounded again, and when he opened it, he found Rabbi Bernstein standing there.

'May I come in, Sean?'

'Of course.'

The old man followed Dillon into the living room. Dillon turned, suddenly anxious. 'She's all right, isn't she?'

'So it would appear. Sean, I don't know all the details, but I know what she'd want me to tell you. She wouldn't want revenge.'

'Well, I do. I'm sorry, Rabbi, but I'm feeling very Old Testament at the moment. An eye for an eye.'

'You love my granddaughter?'

'Not in the way you mean. God knows, she doesn't love me. In fact, she hates what I stand for, but that doesn't matter here. I think a great deal of her, and I don't intend to let the man responsible for her present situation get away with it.'

'Even if she doesn't want that?'

'Yes. So, Rabbi, unless you want to stay for a cup of tea, you'd better go.'

'God help you, Sean.'

The old man went to the door. Dillon opened it for him. 'Sorry, Rabbi.'

Bernstein went out. Dillon closed the door, hesitated, then went back into the living room.

The phone rang. When he answered it, Ferguson said, 'Eleven o'clock tomorrow at my place. I'll expect you.'

139

'I'll be there,' Sean Dillon said, and put the phone down.

The following morning he checked at the hospital and found that she was poorly, but stable. That she was getting the finest treatment in London was a given – Ferguson wouldn't accept less – so there was nothing Dillon could do.

He dressed in dark leathers, a black bomber jacket and white scarf, and took the black plastic urn with him when he left and walked round to Ferguson's flat in Cavendish Place. Kim let him in and Dillon found Ferguson having tea and toast by the fire.

'I didn't have time for breakfast. Blake's on the phone to the President in my study. He'll be with us shortly. Help yourself to a drink. I know you like to start early.'

Dillon did just that, had a Bushmills with a little water. 'Any news from County Down?'

'Oh, Bell's there, all right, and his three cronies, Tommy Brosnan, Jack O'Hara and Pat Costello. Have I got it right?'

'Absolutely.'

Blake came in. 'The President sends his best.

He's very concerned about Hannah. Anything she needs, any kind of special treatment, you only have to ask.'

The front doorbell rang. Kim appeared and looked inquiringly at Ferguson, who nodded and the Gurkha opened the front door. Paul and Kate Rashid were shown in.

She wore a black suit, he was in a leather bomber jacket himself, pullover and slacks. They both seemed cheerful.

'A drink, sir?' Ferguson asked. 'Coffee, tea – something heavier?'

'I'll have what Dillon's drinking,' said Kate.

'Bushmills whiskey, girl, at eleven-fifteen in the morning? You have to be raised to it.'

'Well, I'll have to try, won't I?'

'Suit yourself.' Dillon poured her the whiskey and added a little water. 'Oldest whiskey in the world, they say. Invented by monks in Ireland.'

She took a sip. 'No Superintendent Bernstein this morning?'

'Yes, well, she's lucky to be here at all. She's in the hospital in intensive care. When we got back to my place last night, there was a guy named Ali Salim waiting. I've checked him out. A Party of God fanatic.'

There was silence. Paul Rashid said, 'Is the Superintendent all right?'

'Oh, sure,' Dillon told him. 'She's got a damaged stomach, bladder, spleen, a bullet in the left lung, a chipped spine. Just the kind of thing you expect when some religious fanatic shoots a woman three times.'

Kate Rashid said carefully, 'And this Ali Salim? Where is he?'

'On the table over there.' Dillon nodded to the black plastic urn. 'I brought his ashes for you. Six pounds. That's all that's left.' He poured another Bushmills. 'Oh, didn't I tell you? I shot the bastard after he shot Bernstein.'

She sipped a little of her whiskey, then took a cigarette case from her purse and extracted one. Dillon gave her a light. 'There you go.'

'I'm sorry,' she said. 'About Superintendent Bernstein.'

'Well, you would be, wouldn't you? After all, it wasn't supposed to be her, it was supposed to be me.'

'Really?'

Paul Rashid cut in. 'Why are we here, General Ferguson?'

'Because I warned you before, Rashid, and now

142

I'm telling you outright: If it's war you want, then it's war you'll get. I don't take kindly to my people getting shot. We're going to be over you so closely that you won't have room to breathe, let alone pursue your "alternative target".'

'Really? And who would that be?' Paul Rashid said.

'I can't help but notice that the Russian Premier is in town next month.'

'Is that so?' Paul Rashid told him. 'How interesting.'

'Also too damned obvious,' Dillon said, and lit another cigarette. 'No, he's got something else on the agenda.'

'You'll have to wait and see, won't you?' Paul Rashid got up. 'Come on, Kate.'

It was Blake who said, 'For God's sake, why, sir? Your mother's death was a tragedy, but why take it so far?'

'You're a decent man, Mr Johnson, and yet you still don't see it. The business interests in your country think they can walk in anywhere they like in the world, take over, corrupt, trample on people's rights. The Russians are exactly the same. Well, you won't get away with it in Rashid territory, in Hazar or the Empty Quarter. I have the financial resources to back me up and I have my people. Chew on that, my friend. One thing I'll promise, I'll surprise you.' He turned to his sister. 'Kate?'

Dillon took them to the door and opened it. 'Try and make him see sense, Kate.'

'My brother always makes perfect sense, Dillon,' she told him.

'Then we'll all end up going down the same dark road to hell.'

'An interesting thought,' Paul Rashid observed, and led the way out.

The door closed, and Ferguson said, 'So, we know where we are.'

'Only with him,' Blake said. 'But we don't know the first damn thing about what he intends to do.'

'The ball's in your court,' Dillon said to Ferguson.

Ferguson nodded. 'Let's try the simple approach. We won't get very far trying to listen in to Rashid's phone calls, and coded mobiles make things even more difficult these days, but we'll tap them anyway. We can monitor his travel movements. His planes need a slot, passengers have to be declared beforehand. Special Branch can check them out. Meanwhile, we'll plough through all his friends, all his associates. Maybe we'll get lucky.'

'Sooner rather than later,' Blake said. 'There's an energy to Rashid that I find disturbing.'

'What will you do?' Dillon asked.

'I'm going home. There's a lot I have to talk about with the President. If there's anything you need me for, though, anything at all, just let me know and I'll be back.'

In the car, Paul Rashid pushed the glass divider closed and said to Kate, 'They'll be on our case in every possible way.'

'I know. It'll be next to impossible to get to the Premier now.'

'He was never my alternative, Kate.'

She was amazed. 'But Paul, I assumed it must be.'

'Which is what I wanted everyone to think, and they did, except for Dillon, of course.'

'Then who?'

'For you and you alone: it's the Council of Elders in Hazar, all twelve of them. They're dragging their feet. They're afraid of me, and they don't want me – they distrust my influence with the tribes, and they're right to. Once I dispose of them and am named the Sultan, I will declare a *jihad.* Then all the great powers will have reason to tremble.'

'How do you intend to do it?'

'They'll all be together in two weeks. I want you to go down and base yourself in our office in Hazar. I'll join you later.'

'And how will the job be executed?'

'A suitable bomb, and for that we'll need Bell's expertise, and we'll also need to get you there to talk with him without people knowing. Speak to Kelly. He knows some dodgy people, the kind who do illegal flights in small planes from old RAF airstrips. In and out very quickly. Get it arranged.'

'As you say, brother.'

7

And Kelly came up trumps. He produced a place in Surrey called Grover's Air Taxis, where the proprietor was a shifty-looking middle-aged man in a brown flying jacket and overalls, who met them outside a Second World War Nissen hut, two hangars looming behind.

'Now then, Mick,' Kelly said. 'Let's call this lady Miss Smith and get on with it. As I told you, we need Drumcree. A couple of hours at the most, then back again.'

'No trouble. I can do the old Titan. It's got twin engines and an airstair door.'

'No problem on the approach?'

'None. I'll go in under six hundred from a couple of miles out at sea. There's an old RAF landing strip ten miles out of Drumcree. I'll use my local contact and have a car left there.'

'Good man, then let's go.'

147

'Just a minute. What about my money?'

Kate opened her briefcase, took out a brown paper envelope, and handed it to him.

'Can we leave now?'

Grover hesitated, obviously tempted to look into the envelope, then thought better of it.

'All right.' He turned and led the way to the end hangar, rolled back the door and disclosed the Titan.

'How long will it take?' Kelly asked.

'Hour and a half, depending on the wind.'

'Fine. Let's get on with it,' Kelly said, and ushered Kate through the airstair door.

She called Bell on her coded mobile when they were halfway across the Irish Sea. She caught him in the kitchen of his farmhouse.

'This is Kate Rashid. I'll be with you in an hour.'

'You'll what?'

'I want to discuss your vacation in a much warmer climate.'

'What are we talking about?'

'A big payday. The alternative target.'

'Well, that's for me, sweetheart.'

'Kelly's minding me,' she said, 'We'll see you at the Royal George.'

*　　*　　*

Without bothering to check with Ferguson, Dillon had been following Kate Rashid from the moment she'd left London. Wearing black leathers and astride a Suzuki motorcycle, he'd waited in a small copse and watched Kelly, Kate and Grover through glasses. When they got in the Titan and took off, Dillon drove to the village a mile down the road and went into the pub. There was a log fire burning, but no sign of customers. A middle-aged woman came in from the kitchen.

'My God, it's like a funeral parlour in here,' Dillon said cheerfully.

'It's early,' she said. 'What do you expect?'

'A Bushmills whiskey and directions to Hoxby.' He lied effortlessly and lit a cigarette. 'I was surprised to see a plane take off a little while ago.'

'Oh, that's Mick Grover's outfit. Just up the road in an old wartime feeder station. He does crop spraying, the odd charter flight. Don't know how he makes a living.'

'I don't know how I do.' Dillon grinned. 'You do food?'

'That's right.'

'I'll go and see to my business in Hoxby. I'll probably look in on my way back.'

*   *   *

Grover stayed with the plane, and Kelly drove Kate down to the Royal George. It was quiet enough at that time in the morning, only Patrick Murphy, the barman, reading the Belfast *Telegraph* at the bar. Kelly led the way in.

'Aidan Bell's expecting us.'

'He's in the snug.'

Kate went first and opened the door and Kelly followed. Aidan Bell sat by the fire, smoking a cigarette and drinking tea. He looked up.

'Lady Kate. Now this really does sound interesting. What do you want me to do?'

'What you do best. Twelve Arab sheiks, the Council of Elders in Hazar, are proving a problem.'

'Well now, we can't have that. On the other hand, I'd always understood that the Rashid would follow your brother anywhere. All those wild tribesmen.'

'They will, once the sheiks are taken care of. This one needs the expert touch. It also needs to be a spectacular. Make various people sit up and take notice. You'll need a team, of course.'

'No problem there. I've got some boys.'

'Are they any good?'

'We're all still here, aren't we? And, yes, to answer your question, they won't screw up like Liam. So what's the deal?'

'Rashid Investments has construction interests in Hazar, and I'm flying out today supposedly to supervise them. I want you and your "boys" to turn up the day after tomorrow at Dublin Airport. Our Gulfstream will run you down to Hazar. We'll talk things over more when you arrive.'

'What are you looking for? Some sort of ambush? A bomb? What's your pleasure?'

'We'll discuss that when I see you. Any equipment you need will be down there.'

'So all I have to do is think of the best way of disposing of twelve old Arab sheiks and getting away with my bollocks still intact?'

She laughed harshly. 'True. That last item could be a consideration. We Arabs are terrible people. You must be careful.'

He smiled. 'That I will, Lady Kate. You may be sure.' He raised his teacup. 'A toast. To peace, Lady Kate, to peace.' He took a swallow. 'And stuff it.'

*   *   *

Dillon had shepherd's pie at the pub and a glass of indifferent Sancerre. There were perhaps a dozen people in, locals from the look of them. He finished his meal, paid up and went to his Suzuki. Fifteen minutes later, he was in the copse overlooking the small airfield, waiting.

He sat there, thinking and smoking, sheltering from the light rain, and eventually he heard the sound of engines in the distance and the Titan appeared and turned in for a landing. Dillon watched through his glasses as Kate Rashid, Kelly and Grover talked. Then she and her security man got into her Mercedes and drove away. Dillon waited for a while, then got on the Suzuki and drove down to the airstrip.

In the old Nissen hut, Grover was boiling the kettle on the stove when he heard the Suzuki. He went to the window and glanced out as Dillon got off and pushed the bike up on its stand. The Irishman removed his helmet, left it on the bike and came in, pushing the door open before him.

Grover said, 'What can I do for you?'

'Information,' Dillon said. 'Answers. That kind of thing.'

'What in the hell are you talking about?'

Dillon unzipped the front of his leathers, took

out a Walther with a silencer, and shot the kettle off the stove.

Grover was terrified. 'What's this, for Christ's sake?'

'Well, for starters, you tell me what I want to know and I won't cripple you. So, let's get down to it. The people you just flew out and flew in again. Who were they?'

'Guy called Kelly. I've known him for years. The woman? He said her name was Smith.'

'Really? Where did you take them?' Grover hesitated and Dillon fired on the floor between Grover's feet. 'Where did you take them?'

'County Down. A place called Drumcree.'

'To see who?'

'How in the hell would I know? I flew them in, they left me at the airstrip and drove off to the village. That's all I know. They were back in an hour and a quarter for the return flight.'

'And you didn't hear a word?'

'No. I've no idea what they were up to.'

Dillon raised his Walther again, and Grover jumped. 'I don't know anything, I tell you!' He paused. 'Just that at one point during the flight, they were talking. I heard her say "hazard", "Hazar", something like that.'

'Good man yourself.' Dillon shoved the Walther back inside his leathers. 'Now, let's get one thing straight. What's just taken place is between you, me and my God. No Kelly and no Miss Smith. Are you with me? Because if you're not, I'll come back and blow your right kneecap off.'

'Look, I don't give a damn,' Grover told him. 'Just bugger off and leave me.'

'Don't make me come back.'

Dillon went out, put on his helmet and rode away.

Grover watched him go. 'To hell with them. To hell with the lot of them.' At least he had three and a half thousand pounds in the brown paper envelope.

He opened a cupboard and found another kettle.

Not too far along the road, Dillon pulled into a lay-by and called Ferguson on his mobile.

'Where in the hell are you?' Ferguson demanded.

'Well, if you'll shut up, you old bowser, I'll explain.'

When he was finished, Ferguson said, 'All right, so she went to see Bell and the pilot heard her say Hazar. What does that mean?'

'I have a suggestion,' Dillon said. 'The Rashid house in Mayfair. Did you put in the phone taps yet?'

'Yes. Of course, they haven't said anything. They're too smart for that.'

'Well, it will make him feel confident if we appear to be doing the expected thing. So why don't you get your communications department chaps into the street outside, have them pretend to be working on the telephones, the usual rubbish. In reality, why not instal a directional microphone instead? Who knows? It could pick up some useful stuff.'

'All right, leave it with me. Only, get back here. I need you.'

Dillon went home to Stable Mews and changed. Then he called at the hospital to check on Hannah. The matron gave him five minutes only. She lay there, propped up, festooned with tubes. Dillon sat for a while, then left, angry and bitter. He met Professor Bellamy in the corridor.

'What's the verdict?' Dillon asked.

'Not good, Sean. I think she'll survive, but I can't promise exactly what shape she'll be in.'

'We will travel hopefully,' Dillon said and left.

At Cavendish Place, he found Ferguson going over papers at his desk. 'I've got some interesting news. That directional mike of yours caught a conversation between Rashid and his sister. Rashid said: "You be there to meet Bell and his three cronies when they arrive in Hazar."'

'Did he? Now that *is* interesting. So what do we do?'

'What do *you* do is more like it, Dillon. I'd say Hazar is your next port of call.'

'General, the minute I turn up in Hazar, I'll be in deep trouble.'

'We'll have to take that chance. I can't keep an eye on them without your being down there, being your usual bloody nuisance. I've even found a legitimate excuse for your presence. My cousin, Professor Hal Stone of Corpus Christi College, Cambridge, is, by one of life's coincidences, in Hazar right now, conducting a diving operation on a World War II freighter. With typical university nonsense, he has no real money, so he can afford only a small operation of local Arab divers.'

'Sounds exciting.'

'Actually, it is. What's really interesting is that he's discovered what's left of a Phoenician trading ship partly underneath the freighter. You're a master diver, Dillon. Hal would love someone like you to help out, especially as you won't cost anything. You'd be able to monitor Lady Kate and Bell and company. I'll arrange for your flight, then come down myself once you're settled in. Do you agree?'

'Let's give it a try. There's just one thing. I know these Arab divers. They jump with a stone in both hands. I need another master diver to back me up.'

Ferguson sighed. 'Oh, dear, do you mean who I think you mean?'

'Billy Salter is a first-class master diver.'

'And you think he'll go?'

'Do I think he'll go?' Dillon started to laugh.

At the Dark Man, they found Harry Salter, Billy, Joe Baxter and Sam Hall sitting in a corner booth.

'Jesus, Brigadier, what brings you here?' Harry Salter demanded.

'First of all, it's not Brigadier anymore, Harry. They've made him a Major General,' Dillon said.

'Well, damn my eyes.' Salter waved to Dora behind the bar. 'Get champagne over here, girl. It's a special occasion.'

She found the bottle and came round the bar, but it was young Billy who said, 'What gives, Dillon? You aren't here playing patty fingers.'

'I'm going out to Hazar in the Gulf of Oman, Billy. The General's cousin is trying to work a World War II wreck with bits of a Phoenician ship under it.'

'He's what?' Billy's face was pale with excitement.

'The thing is, he's got no money, Billy, just Arab divers, so I'm going to work for bed and board.'

Billy got up. 'If he needs you, he needs me. When do we go?'

'Tomorrow morning.'

Billy turned to go, but Ferguson said, 'Tell the lad the truth, for God's sake. Last time out he killed four times for us. We owe him.'

Billy turned slowly. 'Is there going to be trouble?'

'Bad trouble, Billy. We're up against rough trade this time.'

'Then you'd better bloody well tell me,' Billy said and sat down again.

Afterwards, he said, 'What a bunch of bastards. I mean, if you're British, you're British. I don't mind this Rashid being half Arab, but you behave yourself. I don't know, Dillon, ever since I've met you, I end up trying to save the world. What time do we leave in the morning?'

'Ten o'clock from Northolt.'

'Who's flying us? Lacey and Parry as usual?'

'Who else could you trust to drop you in from six hundred feet?'

Billy smiled wolfishly. 'Too bloody right. They got an Air Force Cross each last time, didn't they?'

'That's right.'

'Any chance of me getting one?'

'Not in a million years, Billy.'

'And they wouldn't give you one?'

'All they'd give me is twenty years if they could.'

Harry Salter got up. 'Right, we'd better go and get on with the packing.'

'We?' Ferguson said.

'I can't bloody well dive, but I can use a shooter and sit in the boat,' Salter said. 'It's called family.'

At the Mayfair house, Paul Rashid said to Kate, 'Take George. He can act as a link with the tribesmen. He knows the dialect, and they respect him, because he's my brother. They respect you, too, because you're my sister, but they're Arabs. They still feel uncomfortable with a strong woman.'

'Then they must learn.'

He embraced her. 'Bell is what matters. He's good, but he has to obey you. Any trouble, and I'll have him and his three friends wiped off the face of the map. Those are my people there.'

'I know, brother, I know. I won't let you down. I'll astound you.'

Dillon went back to check on Hannah Bernstein. She was slightly more alert and responded to him.

'What are you up to, Sean?' she murmured.

'It's what Rashid is up to. He's recruited Bell to go down to Hazar with his cronies. We don't know what for yet.'

'And you're going?'

'Yes.'

'Tell me about it.'

Which he did.

Afterwards, she said, 'So it's you and Billy and dear old Harry into the war zone again?'

'So it would appear.'

'You'll never stop, will you, Sean?'

'It's what I am, Hannah. I lack a good woman, that's my trouble.'

'Oh, get on with it and stop making excuses.'

'I love you, too.' He kissed her on the forehead. 'God bless, Hannah.'

And for once, she gave him a smile, a real smile, 'God bless, Sean.'

Strange, but there he was: Sean Dillon, the ultimate hard man, and when he went out, there were tears in his eyes.

When he got home, he spoke to Blake Johnson on the phone and brought him up to date.

Blake said, 'Jesus, Sean. Hazar is Rashid territory, and you and Billy and Harry are going to go play deep-sea divers with Ferguson's cousin? Come on, you won't be able to go into a waterfront bar for a drink without someone trying to stick a knife in you.'

'True. All life will be there, Blake. You should come and join in the fun.'

'Frankly, my fine Irish friend, I'm tempted. What are the Rashids up to, Sean? Why import an IRA hit squad into Hazar?'

'Well, that's what I'm going to find out.'

'Then watch your back.'

Dillon laughed out loud. 'That I will, Blake. Who

would have thought it – an IRA enforcer and two of London's finest gangsters in the middle of the desert. Why does it always have to be us?'

'Sean, I'm not into moral philosophy. I just have a sneaking suspicion that you and Billy are going to have much too good a time . . . I dive, too, you know. Do you really think the President . . . ?'

'There's only one way for you to find out.'

At Northolt the following morning, they found Lacey and Parry waiting and, in something of a surprise, Ferguson.

'I thought I'd see you off. Lacey's had the roundels removed, since we needn't advertise the RAF. What are we calling it, Lacey?'

'A United Nations charter, General.'

'Ah, well, no one will quarrel with that.'

The Quartermaster appeared, a rather tall and forbidding retired Guards Sergeant Major. 'There's a question of weapons, Mr Dillon. May we talk?'

'Of course,' Dillon said.

The Quartermaster led the way into an anteroom. On a wide table were several AK-47s, Brownings, Carswell silencers, and three small machine pistols.

'Parker-Hales, Mr Dillon.'

'Excellent, Sergeant Major.'

'I've had diving equipment loaded on board. You'll need air bottles down there. I'd take care if I were you. Never know what these Arab buggers might try to put in them.'

'I take the point,' Dillon told him.

'Good, because I would like to meet you again, Mr Dillon.'

'We'll see what we can do.'

The Sergeant Major said, 'I'll load up, sir.'

While the plane was loading, they drank coffee and tea in the lounge. Ferguson said, 'We have little outright influence in Hazar any longer. All these small countries like their independence these days. They don't have an army, just the Hazar Scouts, a small regiment of Arab Bedu traditionally commanded by British officers. At the moment Villiers is the commander – you know about him.'

'Do I liaise with him?' Dillon asked.

'He could be useful. He has his ear to the ground, knows what's going on. At the moment, as I understand it, the Scouts are patrolling the Empty Quarter. They have problems with Adoo bandits up there, men on the run from Yemen: Lawrence of Arabia stuff. It's just like the old days – any game is better than no game. Just like Northern Ireland, really.'

Billy said, 'The old sod's getting at you, Dillon.'

'Yes, I know he is, Billy, but it's okay.' Dillon smiled amiably. 'What do you want me to do, tell him to get stuffed?'

'Oh, you've been doing that one way or another for some years now, Dillon.' Ferguson got up. 'I don't know what's going on out there, but it's certain to be dodgy. Take care.'

'Ah, but I always do.' Dillon shook hands. 'Don't worry, Charles, you've got me, Billy, and Harry. We're an unbeatable combination.'

A few minutes later, the Gulfstream roared along the runway at Northolt. Ferguson waited, then turned and got into his Daimler and was driven away. It was all up to Dillon now, but then there was nothing new in that.

HAZAR

8

The airport at Hazar was five miles out of town. It was a single runway but had been built by the RAF in the old days for military use, so it was capable of handling anything, even a Hercules. When the Gulfstream landed and they disembarked, two Land Rovers drove up. The man who got out of the first one was in his sixties, deeply tanned, white-bearded, wearing a crumpled bush hat, khaki shirt and slacks.

'Hal Stone.' He held out his hand. 'I understand you're a hell of a diver, Dillon.'

'How did you know it was me?'

'The wonders of modern science. Computers, the Internet, the downloading of pretty colour pictures.' He turned to the others. 'Billy and Harry Salter. What a combination. Even the Kray brothers would have been impressed.'

He called in Arabic and two men got out of the

other Land Rover. 'Load everything. Take it to the *Sultan*.'

Lacey and Parry found them, and Dillon made the introductions. Stone said, 'Are you staying over?'

'Not this time, sir,' Lacey told him.

'Good, then you won't need my rather dubious expertise on Hazar. What to avoid, which on the whole is everything.' He turned to the others. 'Come on. I could do with a cold beer before I show you the *Sultan*.'

In the Land Rover, Dillon lit a cigarette. 'You're actually a Cambridge don?'

'A Fellow of Corpus Christi and Hoxley Professor of Marine Archaeology. There's another thing you should know about me: I used to work for the Secret Security Services when I was a lot younger and rather more foolish. Cousin Charles has filled me in on you and your friends, so I know what you're up to, but frankly I don't care as long as you do some diving for me.'

'Well, that sounds okay,' Billy told him.

'Billy is a master diver,' Dillon said. 'He's good.'

'And you?'

'Okay I'm just modest, and I do have another agenda.'

'A Rashid agenda?' Stone smiled. 'Kate Rashid turned up yesterday with four Irishmen, Northern variety. Should make you feel at home, Dillon.'

'And where would they be staying?'

'The Excelsior Hotel down on the waterfront. It's like a set from an old Warner Brothers movie. All you need is Humphrey Bogart. I said I wanted a cold beer and we'll have it there.' Dillon lit another cigarette and Stone added, 'Give me one.'

'Sure.'

Stone took it and inhaled with conscious pleasure. 'Let me just tell you one thing. What you're up to is your business, but I would like to point out that this is the sort of place where they'll cut your balls off for a packet of Marlboros.'

'The dogs,' Harry Salter said. 'We can't have that, can we?'

There were cottages in the grounds of the Excelsior Hotel. Kate had booked Bell and his three friends into a triple complex around a small courtyard. She herself was staying at the Rashid villa, which also housed the company headquarters and a small computer and communications setup.

A young Arab came into her office and placed

a couple of sheets on her desk. 'A UN plane landed a short while ago. These are the passengers downloaded from the computer.'

Kate had a look and smiled. 'Well, now.'

'Picked up by Professor Stone.'

'Get my jeep. I'll take a run down to the harbour.'

The port of Hazar was small, with narrow alleys and white buildings stepped back up the hillside. The Excelsior, as Stone had indicated, was very old-fashioned, with electric fans turning in the ceiling, a huge marble-topped bar, french windows open to the harbour. There was an assortment of vessels there, a few small coastal freighters, many dhows. Stone pointed to a spot a mile out.

'There's the *Sultan*, the big old dhow. The ship we're looking at, an American ammunition ship sunk by a U-boat on its way to Japan, is about ninety feet down.' They were sitting on the hotel terrace, the awning flapping above them in the wind.

'What's this Phoenician thing?' Billy asked.

'Oh, some of the boys brought up shards of

pottery and various other items. It's down there, all right. What's left of it. I've carbon-dated them. They're possibly from a couple of hundred BC, but you can't be sure.'

'I can't wait to go down.'

'Billy's an enthusiast,' Dillon said.

Behind him, Bell, Brosnan, O'Hara and Costello came into the bar and sat on the high stools. In the moment Dillon saw them in the mirror, Bell saw him. He was totally astonished.

Dillon got up. 'With me, Billy.' He walked over. 'Why, Aidan. You're a long way from Drumcree and all that soft Irish rain.'

'Jesus,' Bell said. 'What are you doing here?'

'Being your worst nightmare.'

Costello, who had just sampled his beer, raised the glass suddenly, but Billy kicked him hard on the right ankle, hooked his arm and removed it from his hand.

'That's very stupid. Do that again and I'll put it in your face.'

A quiet voice said, 'No need for that.'

Dillon turned and found Kate Rashid standing there.

'Why, Kate,' he said. 'And aren't you the wonder of the world? You turn up everywhere.'

They walked back to the terrace, while Stone and the Salters maintained an uneasy truce with Bell and company.

'Bizarre, isn't it?' Dillon said. 'Do you know Stone?'

'Of him. So what are you doing here?'

'I'm diving for him. If you know anything about Hazar, you'll know about the *Sultan*.'

'Oh, I know everything about it, just as I know everything about you and your friends the Salters. You mix in interesting company, Dillon.'

'Very true, Kate. Harry Salter is legitimate now – mostly – but still one of the most influential villains in London. Billy's killed four times. They're not Chesterfields,' Dillon said.

'Yes, and you're not here to spend your time diving for Hal Stone.'

'Oh, yes, I'll dive for the Professor, and so will Billy.'

'And nothing else?'

'Kate, my love, what could there be?'

'You're on my case, Dillon.'

'Beware the heat of the sun, Kate. It can lead to paranoia.' He finished his beer and got up. 'I'll have to love you and leave you. I can't wait to check out that wreck.'

172

She went back to the bar. Bell said, 'What's that little shite up to?'

'There's nothing he can do here,' she said. 'Not a damn thing. This is Hazar. The Council of Elders think they control it, but not for much longer. Soon it will be all Rashid. Now let's go to your bungalow and look at the plans.'

In the living room of Bell's cottage, many papers were stacked on a desk, including a large Ordnance Survey map. Bell said, 'There's only one main road up there.'

'To the Holy Wells, yes.' She nodded. 'And next Tuesday, all twelve of the Council of Elders will be there.'

'You still haven't said how you want it done. Ambush or Semtex bomb? We can do either.'

'I think the bomb would be more persuasive. I'll arrange to have some of my people take you up there, so you can see for yourself.'

'Excellent. But what about Dillon?'

'Oh, I'll take care of that. You know what they say? Diving is a hazardous occupation.'

The wind blowing in from the sea was warm and somehow perfumed with spices as they left the harbour in an old motorboat crewed by two Arabs.

'Christ, Dillon, you don't half bring us to some strange places,' Harry Salter said.

'Come off it, Harry, you love it. It's the edge of danger, this place. You'll need a shooter in your pocket. As the Professor said, you're up against the kind of people who'll cut your balls off for a packet of fags.'

'I'd like them to try,' Salter said. 'I haven't had a bit of action for a while. That *Sultan* looks like something out of an old Sinbad movie.'

Stone laughed. 'You're just about right, Harry, if I can call you that. Its great virtue is that it's big. Lots of cabins on board.'

Dillon breathed deeply of the salt air, and a school of flying fish erupted from the water.

'Jesus, Dillon,' Billy said. 'This is special. I mean, this is the real business.'

They coasted up to the *Sultan*. Someone threw a line, and they tied up and mounted the ladder one by one.

'The boys will take care of things,' Hal Stone said. 'I'll show you your quarters.'

As it turned out, Billy and his uncle were sharing, and Dillon had a cabin to himself in the stern. He unpacked, then checked out the weaponry bag. He laid out the AK-47s on a table, the Parker-Hale machine pistols, the Brownings with the silencers, his own favoured Walther. There was a kick on the door, it opened and Billy and his uncle came in.

'Are we going to war again?' Billy asked.

'Well, we are in the war zone, Billy.' Dillon shoved two Brownings over. 'Loaded plus spare clips. You need something in your pocket here, especially with Bell and company around.'

'Yes, well, screw them.' Harry Salter hefted a Browning. 'Yes, this will do me nicely.' He put it in his pocket, plus the extra clip. 'Loaded for Bell.'

Billy did the same. 'All right, so we've got the heavy artillery here.'

'Only for when it's necessary.'

'At the moment, all I want is to go down to that wreck.'

'Well, let's go out on deck and we'll see.'

There were three Arab divers on deck as Dillon and Billy got ready. Stone was there, and Harry Salter shook his head.

'I don't know, Dillon,' Salter said. 'I mean, it isn't natural, all this diving.'

'You're right.' Dillon was pulling on a blue

diving suit. 'The air we breathe is part oxygen and nitrogen. The deeper I go, the more nitrogen is absorbed and that's when trouble starts.'

He clamped a tank to his inflatable and strapped an Orca computer to the line of his air-pressure gauge. He eased on the jacket with the tank, found a net diving bag and a lamp, then spat in his mask and pulled it on. Billy was doing the same. Dillon made the okay signal with his finger and thumb, and went over the rail backwards, followed by Billy.

Way, way below was a great reef, with coral outcrops, sponges, a kind of blue vault. A crowd of barracuda swam by, there were angel and parrot fish, silversides, horse-eyed jacks. It was a total joy, and Dillon jack-knifed and went down, checking his dive computer for its automatic readings on depth, elapsed time underwater and safe time remaining.

And then, there below, was the freighter, still in very reasonable condition. Dillon turned, made the OK sign to Billy and went down.

He led the way in through a torpedo hole on the starboard side, worked his way through a maze of passageways, emerged through another torpedo hole in the stern and paused. He made a sign to

Billy, thumbs down, and jack-knifed again.

There in the detritus on the seabed under the stern, he hovered and scrabbled with gloved hands and, by a miracle, came up trumps straight away. What he pulled out was a small figurine, a religious figure, a woman with large eyes and a swollen belly.

Billy came close and looked, his expression ecstatic, then he went down himself and started to search. Dillon hovered, then Billy came up with some sort of plate. Dillon nodded and they started up.

Back on the boat, they held their finds out for Hal Stone and stripped off their diving gear. The Professor was delighted.

'Dammit, Dillon, this figurine is a major find. The British Museum would go crazy for it.'

'And what about my plate?' Billy demanded.

'It's a temple votive plate, Billy, and an absolute beauty.'

Billy turned to his uncle. 'There you go. I mean, we've brought up stuff the British Museum would give their eye teeth for.'

'And we've only started, Billy,' Dillon said as he lit a cigarette and turned to Stone. 'We've got visitors.'

*   *   *

Colonel Tony Villiers was a tall, saturnine Grenadier Guardsman in his late forties, many of those years with the SAS. He had soldiered from the Falklands to the Gulf War through countless tours in Ireland. Decorated several times, there wasn't much he hadn't seen, and a tour in Bosnia and Kosovo had compounded it. He sat there in a small motor cruiser now, in headcloth and khaki uniform, a young officer with him, and coasted in to the *Sultan*.

He came up the ladder and Hal Stone greeted him. 'We've met before. I'm Charles Ferguson's cousin.'

'That's a recommendation,' Villiers said. 'And this is Cornet Richard Bronsby, Blues and Royals.'

'So we're still at it,' Hal Stone said. 'Just like the good old colonial days. This is Sean Dillon, by the way, and Billy and Harry Salter.'

'I know about everyone,' Villiers said. 'Charles Ferguson has been very forthcoming.'

A few moments later, sitting in the stern of the *Sultan* under an awning, Dillon said, 'And just how much has good old Charles told you?'

'Enough to indicate that he doesn't know what the Rashids are up to, which is why he's sent you and your friends, Dillon.'

'You and I have been close in the past but never met, thank Christ,' Dillon said.

Villiers said, 'God help me, but I spent enough time chasing you all over South Armagh.'

'Ah, well,' Dillon said. 'I suppose we're off the same side of the street. Is Cornet Bronsby?'

'He's just learning.'

'Good, then let's have a drink and see what the Rashids are up to.'

They pulled beers out of a cooler, and Villiers said, 'Paul Rashid is an old comrade. We did the Gulf together, he got an MC. He's a first-class soldier.'

'Who runs this place,' Dillon said.

'That he does. And, yes, before you ask me, there's little doubt that he's responsible for the Sultan's death.'

'So what would you say they're up to? Why do you bring a notorious IRA terrorist and his team to a place like Hazar?'

'Because you want them to kill someone for you, I'd have thought.'

'But who?' Dillon asked.

'We'll have to see. Unfortunately, I can't stay. We've trouble on the Border from Yemeni Marxists, so Bronsby and I must get back and do a little policing.'

'Stay in touch,' Dillon said.

'You can rely on it. Just one thing.'

'What's that?'

'The youngest Rashid brother, George, the one who was a Second Lieutenant with One Para in Ireland? My spies tell me he's up in the Empty Quarter, operating with the Rashid out of Shabwa Oasis. George not only speaks fluent Arabic but the Rashid dialect.'

'Well, good for him,' Dillon said. 'My Arabic isn't too bad. My Irish is perfect.'

Villiers laughed and replied in Irish, 'I had a grandmother from Cork who used to force it into me when I spent school holidays with her. Good man yourself, Dillon. Keep the faith. Here's my mobile number if you need me.'

Dillon turned to Cornet Bronsby. 'Listen to your man here, son, he's the best. You're in bad company up there, so if you want to live . . .' He shrugged.

Cornet Richard Bronsby smiled, which made him look about fifteen. 'I'd say I've been in extraordinary company, Mr Dillon.'

He held out his hand and Dillon took it. 'Well, as we say in Ireland, watch your back.'

*   *   *

Towards evening, Dillon and Billy decided to dive
again. There was still plenty of light, and it was
warm and the wind gentle as they drifted in. In
the harbour, Kate Rashid sat on the stern deck of
an Arab dhow and watched through glasses. Kelly
stood beside her.

'Dillon and Billy Salter. They're going down
again.'

'What do you want me to do?'

'Kill them now,' she said. 'Take Said and Achmed
with you, and I want no slip-ups, Kelly. There's
too much at stake here.'

'As you say, Lady Kate.'

Dillon pulled on his jacket with his tank and
Billy did the same. Harry and Hal Stone checked
their gear.

'Christ, this is great,' Billy said.

'You've got your knife?'

'Of course I have.'

'Then take a spear gun.'

'Why, Dillon?'

'Because sharks are not unknown in these waters.'

'Really?' Billy laughed. 'Well, you learn something new every day.'

Harry said, 'You bleeding watch yourself.'

Billy grinned, pulled down his mask, and went over. Dillon laughed at Hal Stone. 'What was it Suetonius said, "Those who are about to die salute you"?'

'I could give it to you in Latin,' Stone told him.

'Oh, it's the thought that counts,' said Dillon, and went over the rail after Billy.

There was the blue vault again, that strange feeling of space extending all around them, the freighter below. Dillon and Billy went down together, spear guns in hand. They saw barracudas again, and three or four manta rays down on the bottom. Dillon felt good, enjoying every moment as he dived down, Billy following. They went through the first torpedo hole entry, followed each other through the maze of passages, then emerged through the stern torpedo hole . . . when Kelly plunged down toward them with Said and Achmed, all three clutching spear guns.

Dillon tapped Billy on the back and pushed him away as Achmed fired a spear. It narrowly missed Billy. Dillon jack-knifed, spiralled, fired upwards and caught Achmed in the chest.

Kelly fired his spear and it dropped into Dillon's

left sleeve, a glancing blow that did no damage except to rip the material of his diving suit.

Kelly closed, a knife in his hand, and Dillon grabbed for his left wrist. As they wrestled, Said fired at Billy, who swerved to one side and fired in return. The spear caught Said under the chin.

Dillon and Kelly struggled frantically, then Dillon pulled him round and slashed with his knife across Kelly's air hose. There was a great disturbance in the water, bubbles everywhere, and then Kelly stopped kicking and drifted away.

Achmed struggled to pull the spear from his chest and Billy swerved around him and slashed at his air hose. Then Billy hovered beside Dillon and they watched the three bodies sink below them.

Dillon gave the thumbs-up sign and they started to ascend.

On deck, they sprawled exhausted. 'For God's sake,' Hal Stone said. 'What went on down there? The Third World War? I looked over the stern rail. I could see.'

'We were attacked,' Dillon said. 'A guy named Kelly, ex-SAS. Head of security for the Rashids. The other two seemed Arab.'

'Jesus,' Harry Salter said. 'It must be the bird, that Lady Kate Rashid.'

'Oh, I think you can count on that, Harry. We're an encumbrance, a serious one.'

'Which means only one thing,' Hal Stone said. 'Whatever they're up to here, it's still something that could fail.'

'Yes, I'm inclined to agree with you.' Dillon got up. 'Let's get a shower, Billy, and clean clothes, then we'll go and book dinner at the Excelsior. Who knows who might be there?'

Hal Stone stayed on board as Dillon, Harry, and Billy went to the Excelsior. The bar was not all that busy, and the restaurant was almost empty, Arab workers standing waiting. There were white linen tablecloths, silver, crystal, just like the old days.

They sat in deep chairs by the bar. Dillon ordered a bottle of Veuve Clicquot, then called Villiers on his mobile.

Villiers said, 'Still with us, Dillon?'

'Only just.' Dillon filled him in.

Villiers said, 'It reinforces what I said. Whatever is going on is damned important. Keep me posted.'

They sat talking, and Lady Kate Rashid drifted

into the bar, Bell with her. Dillon got up. 'Watch my back, Billy, Costello's out there on the terrace.'

He walked to the bar, Billy leaned on the other end and looked toward Costello, then he took out his Browning and put it on the bar.

Dillon said, 'They tell me the food's not bad here.'

'It's not Le Caprice, but it's okay.'

'Aidan here would be happier with Irish stew, but you can't have everything. I hope you're not looking for Kelly?' She went very still. 'He rather foolishly attacked Billy and me down on the freighter. It got very nasty. Knives, air hoses being slashed, quite messy. The last I saw of him, he was on the bottom, very dead indeed, along with two Arab divers. Rather stupid, Kate.'

'You shite, Dillon,' Bell said.

'Oh, come on, Aidan, did you want me to roll over and die?'

Bell smiled reluctantly. 'You'd never do that.'

'Never, so if you don't mind, Billy and I will go back to the diving now.'

Bell burst into laughter and turned to Kate. 'And if you believe that, you'll believe anything.'

9

_____

The next day, Bell and his three friends crammed into a Cessna 310 and flew up to a landing strip near Shabwa Oasis, where they were met by George Rashid, who was dressed as a Bedu.

'I'll take you to the road to the Holy Wells,' he said. 'We want you to know the situation exactly.'

He led the way to a triple-benched Jeep, sat in the front with a driver, and Bell and his men got in behind. They drove through the heat, the dust rising.

Costello said, 'What a bloody country.'

'It separates the men from the boys,' George Rashid said. 'And one other thing that's very important for you to understand – this area here, where Hazar borders the Empty Quarter? It's always been disputed territory, which means no one has legal jurisdiction. You could kill the Pope here and no one could do anything about it.'

'Well, that's useful,' Bell said.

They stopped at the main Rashid camp at Shabwa Oasis to refuel and renew water supplies, and took the opportunity to eat.

Costello said, 'What is this?'

'It's goat stew with rice,' George Rashid told them.

Costello said, 'Excuse me.' He went some little distance away and was sick behind a palm tree.

When he returned, George Rashid said, 'Are you all right, Mr Costello?'

'Not really. On the other hand, when you worked South Armagh with One Para, I'll lay odds you ate pub food in every village.'

'Absolutely.' George grinned. 'Irish potatoes and bread and cabbage in season.'

'Screw you,' Costello said. 'You're making it worse.'

Bell said, 'Come on, let's go and look at the site, then we can go back to Hazar and get you an egg sandwich, Pat.'

The road ran through a defile between shallow stone outcrops, and beyond it sand dunes marched away to the horizon. The Jeep pulled in on a slope and George got out.

'That one spot there, below where the road is, is not in the open. It's the obvious place for an ambush. The Holy Wells are ten miles east.'

'Let's take a look.'

Bell led the way into the defile, followed by George and the others. It was quiet down there, the sides of the defile rising three hundred feet.

Bell said, 'We'll make it a line bomb, boys, one side of the road to the other. I'll do it up with Costello. You two can set up with a light machine gun on that ridge. Lay down covering fire. Take out anyone left.'

George said, 'Well, that looks pretty damned good to me.'

'So – we'll go back to Hazar and check on the supplies you have to offer.'

'Whatever you need, you get,' George said and led the way back to the Jeep.

Hal Stone called Dillon, Harry and Billy to the stern deck of the *Sultan* under the awning.

'I've been checking with my local contacts, and George Rashid, Bell and his friends flew up-country in a Three-Ten. Landed near Shabwa, stayed a couple of hours and came back.'

'And we don't know why?' Dillon said.

'I'm afraid not. I have my boys sniffing around for rumours, but nothing's come up.'

Dillon thought about it, then said, 'If we flew up to Shabwa, would it make a difference?'

'As regards finding things out? I'm not sure, and what do you mean by we?'

'Well, for starters, I can fly anything. I don't need a pilot, just a plane.'

'That's interesting. Ben Carver, who owns Carver Air Transport, has two Three-Tens and a Golden Eagle, just for local flights.'

'Fine, so hire me a plane. Harry, Billy, and I will fly to Shabwa and nose around.'

'Well, if that's what you want to do,' Stone said, 'I'll arrange it.'

At the villa, Kate Rashid was working on company papers when her mobile rang. George said, 'I've had word from a source in Hazar, Dillon and the Salters are flying up to Shabwa in one of Carver's Three-Tens. Dillon's piloting.'

'I sometimes think he has a death wish,' Kate said.

'What do we do?'

'I'm getting tired of him, brother. Shoot Dillon and his friends out of the sky.'

'A pleasure,' George Rashid said.

Later in the day, the 310 coasted toward Shabwa, Billy and Harry sitting behind Dillon, the sky a deep blue, the sand dunes, some three hundred feet high, stretching to infinity. Dillon throttled back, eased the control column, slid over an enormous dune and saw below him a column of three vehicles, all crammed with men. The next thing he knew, they were firing at him.

The windscreen and a side window shattered, and Harry cried out as a splinter sliced his right cheek. A burst of machine-gun fire cut into the port wing. Dillon hauled back, banked away, and boosted speed. The column disappeared behind them, but the engines coughed angrily, and then first the port, then the starboard engine, cut out. Silence enveloped them, broken only by the wind.

The sand dune in front was five hundred feet high. Billy said, 'Christ, Dillon, I've never seen anything like it.'

'Well, Brighton Beach it isn't, Billy. Hang on, you two.'

Dillon hauled back on the column, scraped across the ridge and drifted down to a soft sand plain below. The plane bounced a couple of times, wheels up, then ploughed to a halt. Dillon switched off.

'You two okay?'

Salter said, 'That's it. No more foreign holidays. After this, I won't even do a day trip to Calais.'

Dillon got the door open and scrambled out over the wing. Billy and his uncle followed. Harry said, 'What happens now?'

'They'll come looking,' Dillon said. 'If you want my opinion, they knew it was us, if you follow me.'

'So where does that leave us?' Billy demanded.

'Let's see.'

Dillon got his coded mobile out and started to search his pockets. 'Damn! I don't have Villiers's number with me.' He thought a moment. 'All right.' And called Ferguson in London. He got an almost instant reply. 'Charles, it's me. We're in trouble.'

After the explanation, Ferguson said, 'Don't worry, I'll get hold of Villiers. I'll give him your number. He'll handle it. He's as bad as you when he gets stuck in.'

'I'm glad to hear it.' Dillon switched off and said to the others. 'We wait.'

It was only twenty minutes later when his phone rang, and Villiers said, 'Are you all in one piece, Dillon?'

'Absolutely. Myself and the Salters. They were waiting for us.'

'Well, what could you expect? In a place the size of Hazar, they had to know you were coming.'

'So what do we do? They'll find us again before long.'

'I'm forty miles east with the Scouts. I'll leave Bronsby with half of them and come myself with the others, but I'd suggest you move. Check your GPS and let me know your whereabouts.'

'Give me a minute.' Dillon went to the plane and got the required information.

Villiers said, 'Good. Now get the hell out of there. There's an old fort not that far from you that'll be better cover than the plane. Trek northeast. We'll push hard, but they'll be close, Dillon, damn close. Take my mobile number and keep in touch. Good luck.'

Dillon turned to the Salters and told them what Villiers had said. 'Get water, food, an AK each and spare ammunition, then we're out of it.' He grinned at Harry. 'You'll be able to cancel your subscription at the gym, Harry. You'll lose a stone in two days out here.'

It was two hours later that George Rashid and ten Bedu in two Land Rovers found the 310. His chief tracker went sniffing around, came back and pointed northeast.

'That way, *Effendi*, they are on foot.'

'Then run them down,' George said.

The Salters and Dillon walked abreast, wearing headcloths against the intense heat. The problem was finding a way through the dunes. Dillon led, but it was heavy going in the soft sand. They came out into a level plain, and there was the oasis and the remains of a fort.

Billy said, 'Is that a mirage?'

It was Harry who called out, 'Behind you, Dillon.'

They turned and found George Rashid and the two Land Rovers appearing over a sand dune.

'Run for it,' Dillon cried. 'And I mean run. If they catch us in the open, we're finished,' and he stumbled down the hillside.

They dashed past a well, a line of palm trees, and then through what was left of the gateway in the crumbling wall. Dillon led the way up steps to the large wall, where they looked out and saw George Rashid and his ten Bedu arrive.

The Land Rovers came to a halt and the Bedu got out, with George Rashid leading. On the wall, Dillon peered through one of the openings, Billy and Harry on either side clutching their AK-47s.

Harry said, 'What are we doing here? It's like this movie I saw as a kid. Ray Milland, Gary Cooper – *Beau Geste*, that was it.'

'I saw that one,' Billy said. 'When the men were killed, the sergeant put them on the wall to make it look busy.'

'Well, there's only three of us,' Dillon said. 'And we'd better make it good, because these guys really do cut your balls off.'

They took positions and the Arabs spread out from the Land Rovers. Harry Salter said, 'What in the hell am I doing here, Dillon?'

'Having a good time, Harry. Trust me and you'll get back to Wapping.' He took careful aim and fired, and a Bedu went down. 'There you go. We've got plenty of ammunition. Spray the bastards.'

The Rashid retreated behind the Land Rovers

and opened fire heavily on the wall. Dillon and the Salters returned fire.

'Take your time, Billy,' Dillon said. 'Single shot. Let Harry loose off, but you and I take individual targets. That's your strength.'

Billy squeezed off a single round as asked, and a Bedu fell to one side from the shelter of one of the Land Rovers.

'There you go, Billy, that's the way,' Dillon said. 'We hold them back until Villiers gets here.' He took out a pair of Zeiss glasses. There was a flurry of Bedu moves from one Land Rover to another.

Dillon said, 'I just caught a glimpse of George Rashid.'

'So we know where we are with that bleeding lot,' Harry Salter said, and fired a long burst.

Below, George Rashid spoke to his men. 'I want covering fire from one Land Rover. I'll go with four of you in the other, round to the rear. The wall is half fallen there. We take them two ways. Now move.'

A moment later, the Land Rover roared away. Dillon looked again through his glasses and saw legs underneath the other Land Rover. He took careful aim and fired, and another Bedu fell into view and lay writhing on the ground. At the same time, there was a burst of firing from the rear, Dillon turned and George Rashid and his men poured over the broken wall below into the courtyard.

Dillon and the Salters fell down on their faces as automatic fire raked the wall. Dillon and Billy fired back, another Bedu went down, but at the same moment, the men behind the Land Rover at the front gate raked the wall with automatic fire.

Dillon and his friends crouched low as pieces of the wall cascaded over their heads and then there was a burst of firing from some other direction, and Dillon looked out and saw Tony Villiers and his Hazar Scouts come over one of the huge dunes in five Land Rovers. They paused, then opened up with heavy machine gun fire at the Land Rover in front of the fort's main gate. It fireballed as its fuel tank was hit, and the four men left ran for their lives across open ground and were cut down.

Villiers and his men came down the side of the dune, and George Rashid and the three survivors of his group disappeared back over the crumbling rear wall. A moment later, their Land

Rover raced away and disappeared into a narrow defile.

It was suddenly very still. Dillon leaned against the wall with Billy and got a pack of Marlboros out. Harry was slumped down. 'For Christ's sake, Dillon, I'm an old guy.'

'You've done good, Harry.'

'Yeah, I'd be great – if I were the third lead in some old black-and-white movie on a satellite channel. Only you make it happen for real. You're a monster, Dillon.'

The Land Rover column of Hazar Scouts came in through the entrance and halted in the courtyard. Dillon and the Salters went down the steps and Tony Villiers got out of the lead vehicle and approached.

'Hot stuff.'

Dillon shook hands. 'George Rashid was in charge.'

'Really? Then you've definitely hit a nerve, Dillon. You're a lucky man.'

'I'd say that speaks for itself.'

Villiers lit a cigarette. 'Right, I'll take you to Shabwa Oasis. We'll arrange for Carver to find a plane and fly you back to Hazar.'

'That makes sense,' Dillon said.

'And don't forget to thank Charles Ferguson. Without him, you gentlemen would have been dead.'

In the bar at the Excelsior, Dillon sat with Hal Stone and the Salters.

Stone said, 'It really is like a bad movie, Harry.'

'You can bleeding well say that again. A few days away with Dillon isn't like walking up the Palace Pier at Brighton and having fish and chips and a glass of champagne. This one puts you in serious hazard of your life.'

'Oh, come on, Harry,' Dillon said. 'You haven't had so much fun in years and what have you got to worry about? It's Tony Villiers and his boys who're up there taking all that shite.'

Hal Stone said, 'That's all very fine, Dillon, but we still don't have the slightest inkling what the Rashids are up to. The only thing we know for sure is that they want to knock you off, but why? Why are you such a threat?'

'I'd like to know that myself,' Dillon told him.

Billy said, 'If you look at it, the most significant thing is that Bell and his mob are here as a team. What do they need a whole team for?'

'Well, we don't know, do we?' his uncle asked.

There was a moment's silence, and then Hal Stone said, 'Of course, we could always find out.'

They all looked at him, and Dillon said, 'What are you suggesting?'

'Well, there's four of them, including Bell. I assume they must all know what the game is.'

Billy said, 'So if we cut one of them off from the pack, is that what you're saying?'

'Something like that. I don't know. Seems rather obvious.'

'But sometimes the most obvious plans are the ones that work best,' Dillon said.

Harry said, 'What we'd need to know is when these bleeders are available. When they come into town and for what purpose.'

'To get laid,' Billy said.

They all laughed, but Stone said, 'Actually, you're right. I've kept my ear to the ground. One of them, Costello, I think, is apparently quite fond of an establishment named Madame Rosa's.'

'So what do we do, kidnap him?' Harry Salter asked.

Stone said, 'Why not?'

Billy said, 'Okay, so what do Bell and his goons do when Costello turns up missing?'

'I don't know.' Stone shrugged. 'Of course, it's possible they just might think he's in bed with a woman somewhere. Or two.'

'Why, Professor,' Harry Salter teased him. 'I'm shocked, a man of learning like yourself indulging in such unsavoury thoughts.'

'I'll get over it.'

Dillon left the planning of the operation to Harry Salter, and Harry performed brilliantly. That night, he wore an open-necked dark linen shirt, and a cream linen tropical suit, and looked quite affluent.

He sat with Billy at a pavement café on the other side of the road from Madame Rosa's and, thanks to a discreet bribe, waited for word from inside that Costello was on his way. When it came, Harry went in himself – older, well-dressed, wealthy-looking, and had the girls queuing up. Billy waited until he saw Costello arrive, then followed.

Bell and his group sat with Kate Rashid and went over the maps again. Bell said, 'So, we're on line here. The Elders will be en route to the Holy Wells at around noon. We'll fly up tonight in Carver's

Golden Eagle. Sort out weaponry at Shabwa, then carry on by Land Rover in the morning.'

Kate said, 'That sounds good.'

'One change. We'll connect with your brother and his Bedu up there. We may need back-up. Better to have them available.'

'Fine,' Kate said. 'I'll speak to George and arrange it.'

She phoned her brother in London and got nowhere, so she tried his mobile. Paul Rashid answered at once. 'How are things going?'

'Fine. We're going to fly up to Shabwa in one of Carver's planes.'

'I'll see you there. I'm on my way. I'll land at Haman, come on in the Hawk helicopter. Look for me.'

'I will.'

Costello had slipped out of the Excelsior and made his way to Madame Rosa's, where he was greeted with enthusiasm. He had three girls to take care of his every want, Irish whiskey and cocaine to influence him. South Armagh it wasn't. He'd never known such pleasure, and when they took him to a luxurious bedroom, kissed and fondled him a little, then suggested he undress, he was falling over himself. The girls left and Costello started to get ready. The door opened behind him, he turned and Harry Salter came through the door, followed by Billy.

'Here, what is this?' Costello demanded.

Harry had him by the throat. 'Keep your mouth shut. Start dressing again.'

'Now look here.'

Billy took a Browning from his pocket and clouted Costello across the side of the head. 'Just do as the man says if you want to live.'

And Costello, frightened for the first time in years, did as he was told.

They took him out to the *Sultan*, where Dillon and Hal Stone waited. Two Arab deckhands ran Costello into the stern. Dillon barked orders in Arabic. They ripped off Costello's jacket and shirt and then his trousers, leaving him in his underpants. The Salters leaned against the rail, and Hal Stone sat on a canvas chair and drank cold beer, two of his divers behind him.

Dillon said, 'Don't screw me around, Patrick. Bell wouldn't be over here with you lot if you weren't up to something big.'

Costello said, 'Go on, stuff yourself.'

'Oh, I like that,' Harry Salter said. 'I mean, that's elegant. Don't you think that's elegant, Billy?'

'No. Actually, Harry, I think it's rude and stupid and self-destructive.'

'You've been reading those books on philosophy again.'

Dillon said, 'It's a waste of time. I thought there might be some sweet reason here, and obviously there isn't.' He went and picked up a length of chain by the stern rail and handed it to one of the divers. He said in Arabic, 'Round his ankles and over.'

Costello cried out as they put him down and started with the chain. 'Here, what's going on?'

'You're going down,' Dillon told him. 'You can join Kelly and the two Arabs who tried to finish me and Billy off.'

'You wouldn't.'

Hal Stone got up. 'For God's sake, Dillon, you can't do this.' His part in the good policeman/bad policeman routine was impeccable.

'Well, I'm tired of being Mr Nice Guy, Professor. Killing, bombing, you name it, he's done it. He can go for the deep six and who cares.'

He nodded at the two divers. They upended Costello and put him over the stern rail. He screamed in mortal fear and his head went into the sea.

Harry Salter said, 'Pull the bugger back. Maybe he's learned sense.'

Costello lay on the deck, sobbing. Dillon squatted beside him. 'So what's it about, Patrick?'

'I'll tell you, I swear it,' Costello said. 'There's this bunch of Arab leaders called the Council of Elders, and tomorrow morning, they're going to this place called the Holy Wells and we take them out.'

'Dear God in heaven,' Hal Stone said.

'Where?' Dillon asked.

'Rama. It's called Rama.'

Dillon removed his chain, Costello still sobbing. 'Put him in the hold,' Dillon said in Arabic to the divers.

'What did you say? What did you say? Oh God, you're going to kill me,' Costello said, turned and hurled himself over the rail.

He surfaced on the pale yellow stern light and Dillon said, 'Billy.'

Billy took careful aim and shot him in the back of the head.

'Was that strictly necessary?' Hal Stone asked.

'It was if we want the fact that we know what

they're up to to stay private,' Harry Salter told him.

Bell and Kate Rashid waited while Tommy Brosnan and Jack O'Hara went looking for Costello. They came back with no result, and Bell was furious.

'The bastard. I'll cut his balls off. He can't resist skirt. Probably holed up in some whorehouse and drunk.'

'What do we do?' Kate asked.

'We can manage. I'll kick his arse later, but right now let's get moving.'

Ben Carver ran the air taxi firm at the airport. He was fifty, an ex-RAF squadron leader with a DFC from the Gulf War. He was tending to overweight these days. His boys were loading the Golden Eagle. Bell and his men and Kate Rashid approached.

'I heard you lost a plane, Carver,' Kate said. 'A private charter.'

'Yes, a Mister Dillon,' Carver said. 'It crashed in the Empty Quarter, but Colonel Villiers and the Hazar Scouts found them.'

'Well, that's good. I hope you have insurance.'

'Absolutely, Lady Kate.'

'Let's get going then.'

Fifteen minutes later, the Golden Eagle took off, climbed to five thousand and headed for Shabwa.

Dillon caught Villiers on his coded mobile. 'I've got bad news – really bad news – as to why they're here.'

'Tell me.'

Which Dillon did.

Afterwards, Villiers said, 'Have you told Ferguson?'

'No. He should be on his way out here by now.'

'Dillon, I'm a hundred and fifty miles to the south of that road to the Holy Wells and I've split my command, sent Bronsby east. We each have fifty men. I'll never make it.'

'All right. So warn the Council of Elders to turn back.'

'Dillon, it won't happen. They're obviously doing the whole thing on the quiet. These are very old-fashioned people. I tried to speak to the advisers earlier, a routine call, and the mobile phone was out.'

'You mean we sit here and let them drive up

through one of the worst deserts in the world to their deaths?'

'I'll go like hell, but through that terrain, fifteen miles an hour is tops. I'll call in Bronsby for support.'

'That's not good enough.' Dillon thought about it. 'What if we fly to that airstrip at Shabwa?'

'It's surrounded by Rashid Bedu at the moment.'

And Dillon saw it then. 'Leave it. I'll call you back.'

Hal Stone called Ben Carver. 'I heard you'd gone up-country, so you're back?'

'Obviously.'

Stone said, 'I want a flight to a position east of Shabwa, to drop two men by parachute, a thousand-foot job.'

'You must be mad.'

'Ten thousand sterling.'

Carver hesitated and there was silence. Stone looked at Dillon, who nodded. 'All right, Ben, fifteen thousand. Come on, just a one-hour flight, drop them and come back.'

Greed, as usual, ruled the day. Carver said, 'Okay, I'll do it.'

Dillon took the phone. 'Carver? Dillon here. We might need you later to pick up Major General Ferguson from Haman military airfield and take him up-country.'

'Now, look,' Carver said.

'Twenty thousand,' Dillon told him. 'How about that?'

Carver took in a deep breath. 'I've heard of Ferguson.'

'Well, you would. He runs things for the Prime Minister.'

'So it's all kosher?'

'It's just like being back in the RAF, so have the plane ready and two 'chutes.'

Dillon went to the rail where Billy and Harry were having coffee.

'So what gives?' Harry asked.

'This is me and Billy,' Dillon told him.

Billy said, 'Come on, Dillon, what are we into now?'

'I've spoken to Villiers. He's split his command. He'll drive hard through the night, but it's a hell of a way to cover at fifteen miles an hour. Besides that, that airstrip at Shabwa is in Rashid hands. The Council of Elders seem to have a security blackout, according to Villiers.'

Hal Stone said, 'So they'll simply drive through the night to certain death some time tomorrow morning.'

'That's not the way I see it.' Dillon turned to Billy. 'In Cornwall last year, you did brilliantly. Jumped from six hundred feet without any training. Somebody should have given you wings.'

'Here, come off it, Dillon,' Harry said. 'You're talking about jumping from a plane up there? The two of you trying to screw things up until Villiers and his cowboys get there? Am I right?'

'Harry, it's what I'm doing. Billy's a free spirit, and Billy and I share a love of philosophy.'

'What in the hell is that supposed to mean?'

'Plato. Remember him, Billy?'

And Billy Salter, London gangster, four times in prison, a killer in his time, smiled the coldest smile possible. 'Sure, I remember: "The life which is unexamined is not worth living". Which means to me: the life not put to the test. Time to put ourselves to the test, Sean.'

'Good man yourself. I'll fly up with Carver in his Golden Eagle, just like Cornwall, Billy, except it's headfirst at one thousand feet in this case. Some say I'm mad, Billy, unhinged, you might say. I've done bad things in my life, but the Rashids have done worse and I'm going to stop them.'

'No, you've got it wrong, Dillon,' Billy said. '*We* are going to stop them.'

'Billy, you're mad, too,' Harry told him.

'What else do I do? Go home to Wapping? Chase birds, get so frustrated I finally do one job too many and pull five years?' Billy smiled. 'I'd rather go down for something worthwhile.'

Harry Salter was astonished. 'What can I say?'

'Nothing,' Dillon said. 'Just come along for the ride.'

10

In London, Charles Ferguson was clearing his desk when the doorbell rang, and Kim showed Blake Johnson in.

'Good to see you, Blake.'

'The President wanted me here. This latest news has shocked him greatly.'

'You realize, Blake, that Hazar is neutral. The border with the Empty Quarter is disputed territory. You could have a war there, butcher the Council of Elders, do what you like and be totally untouchable by any other country.'

'Yes, we know that, Charles, but the ramifications would be far-reaching.'

'Which is why the President has sent you?'

'Yes.'

'And has spoken to the Prime Minister.'

'So I believe.'

'Well, we're going to Downing Street to speak to

him now. You've done well, Blake – the President and the Prime Minister on the same day.'

At the door of the most famous address in the world, an aide greeted them.

'General Ferguson, Mr Johnson. The Prime Minister is waiting.'

He took them upstairs, past the pictures of previous Prime Ministers, knocked and opened the door of the Prime Minister's study. He was working at his desk in shirtsleeves, the youngest Prime Minister for more than a century. He glanced up, the face firm, and then smiled in a familiar way.

'General Ferguson.' He got up, came round the desk and shook hands. 'And Mr Johnson? About time.' He clapped Blake on the shoulder. 'The President has brought me up to date. I'd like to hear it from you two.'

Later, someone brought tea and coffee, and the Prime Minister sat there, his face very calm. 'It defies belief that the Rashids would behave in such a way. I know the Earl well.'

'It's a fact, Prime Minister,' Ferguson said.

'It's appalling. He tries to assassinate the President and now the Hazar Council of Elders.' The Prime Minister turned to Blake. 'Would you agree with me that this would be a disaster?'

'In our opinion, sir, that's exactly what it would be.'

The Prime Minister sat there, face calm, brooding. 'Well, you may act with my full authority.' He stood up. 'I have another appointment. Do what you have to do, General.'

They were ushered out. It was over.

Ferguson said, 'Hazar next stop, Blake.'

In Hazar, Kate Rashid and Bell had landed at the airstrip near Shabwa. Four hours later, they were waiting for the Rashid Gulfstream at the military base at Haman. Early in the Southern Arabian dawn light, the plane glided down and several Land Rovers moved forward. Kate got out of the first one, wearing a khaki bush shirt and slacks and an Arab headcloth.

Paul Rashid embraced her. 'Where's George?'

'With his men on the road to the Holy Wells, with Bell and his people. Is Michael well?'

'Holding the fort in London.'

Rashid warriors had emerged from the Land Rovers and stood there with their rifles in total silence. Kate turned and snapped her fingers. A young boy ran forward, holding a robe, helped

Paul Rashid into it, and then offered a headcloth. Rashid fastened it, then turned and raised his right arm, fist clenched.

'My brothers,' he called in Arabic, and put his arm around Kate.

They brandished their rifles and roared approval.

'So, let's get on with it.' He helped her into the lead Land Rover and got in beside her.

He lit a cigarette. 'So, Bell and his team are definitely on schedule?'

'Yes. As I told you, George and his warriors are supporting them. The only problem is that one of Bell's men went missing. A drunk and a womanizer. They tried to find him, but Bell thinks he's holed up in some whorehouse.'

'I don't like that. When a pattern is disrupted, I wonder why.'

'Well, he's that kind of guy, Paul.'

'And Dillon?'

'Still on the *Sultan* with Professor Stone and the two London gangsters.'

'Totally out of their element.'

'Whatever Hazar is, it's not Wapping. Over there they are something, here they are nothing.'

'True.' Paul Rashid brooded. 'And Shabwa is ours?'

216

'Absolutely. Dillon couldn't fly up there and land even if he wanted to.'

'And why should he? He doesn't know what's going on.' Rashid nodded. 'So, I go with an escort, to the Holy Wells ambush site, join George and his men and Bell.' He turned and smiled. 'Would you come with me?'

'It'd be a privilege, brother.'

'Good.' He lit another cigarette. 'We'll set the world on fire, little sister.'

She took his hand and held on tight.

At the airport, just after dawn, Carver checked out the Golden Eagle. Hal Stone was there with Dillon and the Salters. Dillon had opened the weaponry bag from London, the best the Sergeant Major could supply. Titanium bulletproof waistcoats, AK-47s, a couple of Brownings with silencers, half a dozen fragmentation grenades, two Parker-Hale machine pistols.

Dillon and Billy got kitted out. Carver said, 'What's going on here?'

'Are you still on the RAF Reserve?' Dillon asked.

'So what?'

'Well, you've got a DFC. After this, you might get

another one. We're the good guys, Ben. Your guys. Does that give you a problem?'

Carver's smile was instant. 'No, it bloody well doesn't.'

'So let's do it.' Dillon turned. 'Are you coming, Harry?'

But it was Stone who said, 'Dillon, they won't believe this at high table at Corpus – but I'm coming, too. Billy was right. A life not put to the test is not worth living.'

Up in the high country, Bell, O'Hara and Brosnan worked on the road through the defile, laying packs of Semtex, stretching wires to a detonator. It was early, the real heat of the day still to come. Bedu squatted and watched. George Rashid crouched close by.

Bell said, 'Funny, isn't it? Back there in South Armagh, you were trying to stiff us.'

'Of course I was. I held Her Majesty's commission as a Second Lieutenant in One Para. You were the enemy. I shot two of your people personally.'

'Bastard,' Brosnan snarled.

Bell said, 'Don't be silly. He was doing his job. Now get on with the wiring.'

An hour and a half earlier in the dawn light, Carver had flown in at five thousand feet and descended. Dillon leaned over his shoulder.

'Is that it?'

'Rama, that's all I know.'

'Go down and let's make sure they're not there.'

The Golden Eagle descended to a thousand feet. Carver said, 'It looks clear to me.'

'Good. Go round again and we'll jump.'

'You're crazy, you know that?'

'Yes, but it does make life interesting, Ben.'

Dillon went back and nodded to Billy. 'Time to go. Get the door open.'

It was Harry who moved first as he wrestled with the locking bar. The airstair door opened, the steps went down and there was a huge intake of air. Stone and Harry hung on and Billy and Dillon moved forward, the AK-47s and Parker-Hales across their chests.

'After you,' Dillon shouted above the roaring. 'You're a younger guy.'

Billy laughed. 'You're an older guy, so I'll be on the ground first to protect you.'

He stepped out onto the airstair door, went headfirst and Dillon went after him. The Golden Eagle started to turn away, and Stone and Harry wrestled with the door and finally got it closed. Harry ran to a window and, as they banked, saw the two 'chutes land way below.

'They made it.'

'Good,' Professor Stone said. 'So let's get out of here before the other people notice us and start asking questions.'

At Northolt, Ferguson had found Lacey and Parry waiting with the Gulfstream, plus the Sergeant Major with two AKs and four Brownings.

'You're going into battle again, General?' he said.

'Well, it's not exactly good where we are going, so let's be ready.' He turned to Blake. 'You can handle an AK?'

'Charles, that's like asking if your grandmother can cook. I was in Vietnam.'

Ferguson shook hands with the Sergeant Major and turned to Lacey.

'Four Brownings, Squadron Leader. That's one

each for you and the Flight Lieutenant. Hazar may prove a serious problem as regards your health. I thought you should be ready.'

'Very considerate of you, General,' Lacey said. 'We've got a young lady on board to handle catering. Flight Sergeant Avon.'

Ferguson turned to the Sergeant Major. 'Find another Browning.'

'Of course, sir.'

Later, sitting in the plane, the door closed, ready to go, the young Flight Sergeant appeared, not wearing an RAF uniform but an international-looking navy blue job.

As the plane moved away, she said, 'Anything you gentlemen would like?'

'Later, Sergeant.' Ferguson smiled. 'You know who I am?'

'Of course, General.'

He picked up the extra Browning the Sergeant Major had given him. 'I presume you've had basic weapon training?'

'Of course, sir.'

'Good. Take this. We're going into harm's way. I'd like to think you can defend yourself if needs be.'

She was so cool, he could feel the ice. 'That's very good of you, General. I've got prawn salad,

Lancashire hotpot, smoked salmon and game soup.'

'Sounds fine,' Blake said.

Ferguson smiled. 'Mr Johnson works for the President of the United States, but do be prepared to use the Browning. The people on the other side aren't nice.'

'No problem, sir. I've a bottle of Tattinger in my fridge if you'd care for a glass of champagne.'

She left. Blake said, 'I wonder how it's going for Dillon?'

'The question should be, how is it going for the other lot,' Ferguson said.

On the ground, Dillon divested himself of his 'chute, covered it with soft sand and went looking for Billy. He clambered up the nearest sand dune and found him below on his knees, burying his parachute. Dillon ploughed down to join him.

'You're okay?'

'Fine,' Billy told him. 'We should do this more often.'

Dillon took out his mobile and called Villiers. The Colonel replied almost instantly. Dillon said, 'Billy and I are on the ground in one piece.'

'Any sign of the opposition?'

'Not when we flew over. We'll make for Rama, see what the situation is on the road. Where are you?'

'Twenty miles.'

'And Bronsby?'

'About thirty miles, maybe forty, to the east.'

'Good. Billy and I will push hard and cut the road. The minute I get a smell of them, I'll call you.'

He stuffed his phone into a pocket of his bush shirt, turned to Billy, took out a compass and checked it.

'Right, let's move it. Once we find the road, we'll climb one of the dunes and see what we can see.' He took a headcloth from his backpack and pulled it on. 'Do the same, Billy, it's going to get hot.'

They cut the road an hour later and moved along it at a half run. There was a fine covering of sand, but no sign of tyre tracks, no sign of anything. Finally, Dillon stopped. The defile was before them.

'This has got to be it. Let's go up there.' He pointed to a sand dune that was at least five hundred feet high. 'We'll see anything that's coming.'

It was hard going, the heat increasing as they toiled up the steep side of the dune, and then they were on top and sat down. Billy produced a bottle of water, drank some and passed it to Dillon, who drank deeply, then took out his Zeiss glasses and scanned the horizon.

'That's it.' He pointed and passed the glasses to Billy. 'They're to the east, the farthest part of the road.'

Billy looked, adjusted the glasses and the lead Land Rover sprang into view, the column behind.

'Jesus,' Billy said. 'The Rashids are coming up fast.'

'I'd say you're right, Billy.'

'And two of us.'

'Let them get closer, then I'll call in and let Villiers know where we are.'

Down in the defile at Rama, Bell, O'Hara and Brosnan worked on their bomb. George Rashid sat waiting with some of his men. Up above on the edge of the defile, a handful watched. Suddenly, one of them fired a shot into the air, stood up and waved. A moment later, two more Land Rovers appeared and braked to a halt. Paul and Kate Rashid got out.

Rashid went forward and spoke to Bell. 'So, it goes forward?'

'It will if we can get on with it instead of having a lot of idiots in bed sheets interfering.'

Beside him stood a plastic bottle of water. Suddenly, there was a single shot and the bottle jumped into the air. Two of Paul Rashid's guards ran forward and pulled him and Kate to one side, turned them, and ran them to the Land Rover column. There was another shot and one of them, a bullet in his back, fell on his face.

On the top of the sand dune, Dillon looked through the glasses. 'It's Paul Rashid down there and Lady Kate. Who wrote *this* script?'

'I don't know, Dillon. What I do know is there's forty down there and two up here.'

'So live dangerously, Billy. I'll take the one on the left doing the wiring. You do the one on the right.'

He took careful aim and shot O'Hara, who had stood up, in the back. Brosnan was running, weaving, toward the column, and Billy got him in the lower spine, driving him forwards onto his face.

*   *   *

Paul Rashid looked up to the top of the sand dune, calm, controlled, adjusting his glasses, and caught a glimpse of the two men.

'Dear God, it's Dillon.'

He turned and called to his men as Bell arrived. 'Surround the dune,' he said in Arabic. 'And I want them alive.'

Dillon got his mobile out, called Villiers and brought him up to date.

Villiers said, 'Won't be long now, but can you hold?'

'There's two of us, Colonel, that's all.'

'Just hang on there, Dillon, I'll push like hell.'

'And Bronsby?'

'Trying just as hard from the other direction.'

'Well, I hope you all make it. They're coming up to get us right now.' He put the phone back in his breast pocket. 'Here we go, Billy.' He took careful aim and started to shoot at the Arabs climbing the dune.

Billy joined him. 'Listen, Dillon, if the Council of Elders lot turn up, all this shooting's going to put them right off.'

'Exactly, Billy. Let's pray Colonel Villiers gets here soon.'

But Villiers had done better than that. He cut the road ahead of the Council of Elders convoy, stopped them and spoke to their escort commander. The convoy turned and went back. Villiers carried on to Rama with his men.

Dillon and Billy burrowed in, confident of only one thing: they had the high ground. They shot several of the Rashid Bedu as they came up the sand dune, but they were still only two . . . and then in the far distance on the road, Villiers appeared.

One of Paul Rashid's men ran to his side and pointed. Rashid turned, focused his glasses and saw Tony Villiers in the lead Land Rover.

'Damn,' he said to Kate. 'It's the Hazar Scouts.'

'So, all we have down there is a totally useless bomb,' Kate said.

'Let's get out of here,' Paul Rashid said. 'And live to fight another day.'

His men retreated to the column, some firing up

at the top of the sand dune. Billy and Dillon fired back, and then the column moved away and turned out into the desert.

Dillon lit a cigarette and checked the approach of Villiers and his men. 'Just in time, isn't that the phrase?'

They went down and found Villiers, as the Land Rovers rolled to a halt. Dillon said, 'We've got a bomb here. If you've got a pair of wire cutters, I'll take care of it for you.'

'So kind.' Villiers spoke to one of his men in Arabic. After a while, Dillon was supplied with what he needed.

Later, they sat beside the lead Land Rover, drank bitter black tea and smoked cigarettes.

'So, the Elders are safe,' Villiers said.

Dillon produced a pack of Marlboros and lit another one, Tony Villiers reached over and helped himself. 'I'll tell you, I may have commanded that man in the Gulf, but I'd still like to know what goes on inside his head.'

'Rashid?' Dillon said. 'Tell me, Colonel. You did Irish time. Remember Frank Barry?'

'Who could forget?'

'He also had a title. An Irish Peer, the Lord of Spanish Head up there on the Down coast, pots of money. But all that was important was what went on in his head. The game.'

'And you think that's true of Paul Rashid?'

'He's done everything else. He's got everything else. Yes, I'd say the one thing he's seriously left with is the game.'

'So, Bosworth Field is Rama today.'

It was Billy, the London gangster, who said, 'Dauncey, that was the family name?'

'That's right,' Dillon said.

'Well, they lost with Richard III and they lost with us.'

Dillon sat there thinking about it, then smiled. 'True, Billy, very true. Are you trying to make a profound point?' He turned to Villiers. 'Billy and I share a love of moral philosophy. So does Paul Rashid.'

'What I find really interesting is Sean Dillon, pride of the IRA, loving moral philosophy.'

'You didn't approve of my cause, Colonel, but I was just as much a soldier as you, and you know damn well that soldiers go beyond position, beyond money, beyond normal success. They stand up and take the sword.'

'To hell with you, Dillon,' Tony Villiers said. 'You're too damn good.'

They started west now, following the tracks of Rashid's column, and gradually the light changed, things got darker. Some miles away, Cornet Bronsby of the Blues and Royals approached with his men toward an improbable rendezvous and was suddenly under fire.

They responded at once. There was an exchange. The column they had reached head-on was Paul Rashid and his group on the retreat from Rama.

There was a brief return of fire, but Rashid's men held them off. Then Bronsby decided enough was enough and ordered his men to retreat. At some time in the confusion, men rushed in from the shadows and overwhelmed him.

Paul Rashid, his sister and Bell pushed south and finally made contact with George Rashid, and discovered Bronsby. Paul Rashid was not happy. He sat there with Kate and George and Bell, and Bronsby was brought forward.

In a way, it was like being back at Sandhurst. This young decent Englishman was a soldier simply doing his job. In many ways, so like Rashid. It was a kind of turning point he couldn't really explain to himself. All he knew was that this wasn't the way it was supposed to have happened . . .

'I know where they are,' Villiers said to Dillon. 'My spies out ahead are earning their money. One of their wounded has confirmed that they've caught Bronsby.'

Dillon said, 'That isn't good, is it?'

'No. They're a very cruel people by nature. What you and I think of as horrific, they think of as normal in a strange kind of way.'

Dillon said, 'So they're going to give him a hard time.'

'I'm afraid so.'

Dillon sat there, smoking a cigarette and thinking about it.

'I don't like that.' He said to Billy, 'Bronsby is what you'd call a posh git, but he was just doing his job.'

'Yeah, well, I don't like it either.'

He turned to Villiers. 'So where do we go?'

'I'd say Shabwa.'

'And what do we do? Take Rashid and the good Kate on face-to-face?'

'To a certain degree.' There was a pause and Villiers said, 'You like her, Dillon.'

'Who the hell wouldn't?' Dillon laughed and lit another Marlboro. 'Go and stuff yourself, Colonel, and let's press on, just in case we can help Bronsby.'

11

Outside Shabwa Oasis, cooking fires glowed and the Rashid Bedu held the high ground. Villiers and his men were exhausted, but they had enough energy to make something to eat. And then the screaming started. It was just after midnight and continued at intervals.

Up there on the hill, Paul Rashid, George and Kate approached to where Cornet Bronsby was tied down.

Kate said, 'Is this what you want, brother? He was one of your own, a Guardsman.'

'Yes, but that isn't the point.'

'It doesn't bother you?'

'It bothers me a great deal,' he said bitterly, 'but other things are more important.'

*   *   *

A full moon bathed the mountainside in a harsh white light. The men of the Hazar Scouts waited impassively behind what cover there was. They smoked cigarettes and drank the English version of coffee provided in self-heating cans.

Tony Villiers sat behind a boulder with Dillon and Billy, drank tea and topped it up with Bushmills whiskey from a bottle provided by his servant Ali.

'This suit you, Dillon?'

'Perfectly.'

'Not me. I don't drink,' Billy told him.

Villiers said to Ali in good Arabic, 'I'd offer you one, but I know the Prophet forbids it.'

'But the Prophet, whose name be praised, is always understanding,' Ali told him. 'And the night is cold.'

'Then two whiskey sups,' Villiers said. 'One for you and the other for the radio operator.' He nodded to Aziz.

Ali passed the bottle to Aziz, who restricted himself to one swallow, then passed it to Ali, who wiped the neck and had a drink.

Above them there was another scream. It faded away. Billy said, 'What are they doing?'

Ali said, 'The skin – they slice the skin, *Sahb*. His masculinity they take later.'

The screaming started again.

'I could do with another,' Dillon said.

Villiers splashed Bushmills into the Irishman's cup. Billy said, 'It's enough to make me ask for one, but I won't. What I'd like to do is put a bullet in Paul Rashid.'

Villiers said to Ali, 'You know the *Sahb* up there is twenty-two years?'

'A baby, Colonel.'

The radio crackled. Aziz listened, then turned. 'Visitors, *Sahb*, a British General named Ferguson and two others.'

'Excellent. Make sure your people are alerted.'

Coming up the hill in a Jeep, Ferguson, Blake and Harry Salter wore combat gear and Arab headcloths. The Jeep paused in the shadows and the three men got out. Billy went forward and his uncle put an arm around him.

'So you made it, you young bastard? I hear it was a load of shit. You must be rivalling Billy the Kid.'

'You look interesting.' Billy smiled. 'You didn't get that lot in Savile Row.'

'Billy, I feel like I'm an extra in a Christmas pantomime at the Palladium.'

'Blake Johnson, Colonel Tony Villiers,' Ferguson said, and there was a cry of agony from above. Ferguson was horrified. 'Who's up there?'

'Cornet Richard Bronsby, of the Blues and Royals, Second Lieutenant in the Household Cavalry. He could have been riding around London in a breastplate and helmet. Instead, he's out here being tortured to death by Rashid Bedu.'

The scream that followed was prolonged and appalling. Villiers added, 'I wish we could interfere, but there are too many of them and they have the high ground.'

And up there, Paul Rashid, Kate, George and his men waited beside their own fires, and beyond, in the shadows, Cornet Richard Bronsby lay stretched out and endured torment.

Aidan Bell sat beside the fire, shivering, drank whiskey and smoked a cigarette. Paul Rashid crouched beside him.

'I want you out of here. The staff will expect you at South Audley Street. The Russian Premier arrives in London next week. I'll be hard on your heels. Work something out.'

'Jesus, wasn't Nantucket enough for you? Wasn't this?'

'No, not until I get my revenge. Not until I am satisfied. Land Rovers will take you. Leave now and work fast. I want a plan ready when I get there.'

He stood up and walked away and joined Kate and George at the fireside. She was upset; the screams from Bronsby were hard to take.

'Paul, is this necessary?'

'My people expect it, Kate. It is hard, but it is what they expect.'

She sat there, unhappy, upset. Bronsby cried out again, quite dreadfully, on and on before stopping.

Ali said, 'I think he has gone, *Sahb*.'

Villiers sat there brooding about it. Ferguson said, 'Dear God.'

Dillon turned to Blake. 'Well, there you go. It must remind you of the joys of the Vietcong in the Mekong Delta.'

Harry Salter said, 'And we let people like these into the country.'

Dillon managed a hard smile. 'Why, Harry. You're a racist.'

Villiers picked up an AK. 'All right. That's enough, Ali, let's take a look. I've waited long enough.'

Dillon said, 'Would you mind some company?'

Villiers hesitated, then said, 'I suppose that at the end of the day we are from the same side of the street. Let's do it.'

They went up the hill, Villiers, Dillon, Billy, Harry, and Blake, and they found Cornet Bronsby pegged out. He was quite dead, his skin peeled down from the chest, his private parts stuffed in his mouth.

'There was no need for that, *Sahb*,' Ali said. 'I am ashamed. There is no honour in this.'

He was carrying an old British Lee Enfield bolt action rifle. As he turned to lead the way, he stumbled, tripped and fell over, the rifle flying from his hands. Dillon helped him to his feet and Villiers picked up his rifle.

Ali held his arm. 'Ah, it's bad, *Sahb*, maybe broken.'

'We'll see,' Villiers told him. 'We'll go back to the camp. Tell half a dozen men to carry him down, but tell them to be careful.'

'No need, *Sahb*. The triumph up on the hill is in what they have done. They will kill no more. We are of the blood. I know.'

'Well, I'm not,' Dillon said.

They brought Cornet Richard Bronsby down the

mountainside to the camp and loaded the corpse into a body bag and onto a Land Rover.

Ferguson had a look. 'Why on earth would they do such a thing?'

Villiers said, 'This kind of mutilation is a warning. With all respect to Dillon, I've seen as bad in Ireland.'

Dillon lit a cigarette. 'He's right, but he's wrong in one respect. I was IRA for more than twenty-five years. I killed soldiers, I killed Loyalists, but always as a soldier, never like this.' He turned to Villiers. 'They'll taunt you as the sun comes up, you know that.'

Villiers nodded. 'And that will be five hundred metres away. It's a funny thing, Dillon. I was never much good with a rifle. That's why I used Ali. Now, he's cracked his arm, and in the morning, they'll stand up, scream and shout, and give us a hard time.'

Dillon smiled. 'I hope they do, Colonel, I hope they do.' He picked up Ali's Lee Enfield. 'My grandfather used one of these in 1917 in the trenches of Flanders. He was awarded a medal for bravery in the field. It's a bolt-action, single-round, Three-oh-Three.'

Tony Villiers lit a cigarette and passed the packet

across. 'I also remember that the preferred weapon of IRA snipers in South Armagh was the Lee Enfield.'

'Well, I'm from County Down myself, but I would agree with you,' Dillon said.

In the morning, Dillon, Ferguson and the others drank coffee as light filtered through. The orange globe of the sun slowly arose, suffusing the dawn light.

Suddenly, six figures appeared on the hill five hundred metres away. Dillon looked through the Zeiss glasses. Paul Rashid sprang into view, George and three Bedu and Kate with him.

'Guess who,' Dillon said and passed the glasses to Villiers.

Villiers said, 'Christ.'

One of the Scouts was behind him holding Ali's Lee Enfield. Dillon snapped his fingers and said in Arabic, 'Now.'

On the hill, Paul Rashid looked through his own glasses. 'It's Dillon,' he said. 'Tony Villiers and Ferguson, Billy Salter and his uncle.'

One of the Scouts passed Dillon the Lee Enfield. Dillon secured its belt around his wrist. And then, for some perverse reason, he fired to miss, kicking up sand between Paul Rashid's feet. Rashid dived for cover, pulling Kate with him. Then Dillon shot the man on the end of the line, then shot another one.

Ferguson said, 'They're running scared, Sean. We'll have a go back home in London. Leave it.'

'Like hell I will. I've just shot those two. I'll make it four. Watch.'

He took number three, then four, and four was George Rashid.

It was quiet, and on the ridge Kate fell on her knees in horror. Paul said, 'Leave him,' and grabbed her hand. 'Come with me now.'

They made it to a Land Rover and departed. Villiers led the way up the hill. The four Arabs were all very dead, eyes staring, arms outstretched.

Villiers said, 'You're one hell of a marksman, Dillon.'

Harry Salter said, 'Christ, they should call you the Executioner.'

Villiers and Ferguson were looking at the four Arabs, and it was Ferguson who said, 'Dear God, this one is George Rashid.'

'Have we got a problem?' Dillon asked.

'Well, Paul Rashid won't be pleased.'

'Neither will Mrs Bronsby, so stuff Paul Rashid and his bloody money.' Dillon stood up and walked away.

At the Rashid villa at the port, Kate Rashid stood in a shower letting the heat soak into her, a futile attempt to make herself feel better. She had lost a brother, but more than that, this girl who was half English aristocrat, an Oxford MA, had been forced to confront Bronsby's truly dreadful torture.

She dried herself, pulled on a robe and went out. Paul Rashid sat by the open french window, working his way through papers. He looked up.

'How are you?'

'How should I be? George is dead.'

'Yes, and it was Dillon who killed him. Do you still like him, Kate?'

'We killed Bronsby, and in a terrible way.'

'True, and the good book says an eye for an eye. I don't mean the Koran, I'm referring to the Bible.'

'So now we get home to what?'

'We don't go home, not yet. This is Hazar. I still rule the Rashid, not the Council of Elders.

The attempt was in the Empty Quarter, disputed territory. No one can touch us.'

'So what do you intend, brother?'

'Dinner at the Excelsior. If I were a gambling man, I'd say that's exactly where our friends will go this evening. I think that of all of them, it's Dillon who will expect it. You know I love old movies. So often they depict life in a way life itself doesn't.'

'So what happens? There's a confrontation, guns are pulled?'

'Not necessarily. What happened to me at Shabwa?'

'The assassins?'

'These people are always available. They take *quat*, they would kill their grandparents for the right price. If we take out Dillon and his friends, to a certain degree it pays for George.'

'And afterwards?'

'We return to London.'

'To what?'

'Oh, I'll think about it. Now get dressed. Wear a nice frock and we'll go to the Excelsior and see if I'm right.'

*   *   *

On the *Sultan*, they sat under the stern awning and had a drink.

Ferguson said, 'What happens now, Tony?'

Villiers said, 'You can't touch him, but then you know that.'

'We couldn't even touch him in Manhattan,' Blake said.

Dillon nodded. 'Or London.'

Ferguson asked, 'So what happens?'

There was a sudden flurry of rain and Ali, who had accompanied Villiers, reached for a bottle of champagne, his left arm in a sling, and refreshed the glasses.

Dillon said, 'I'd ask Harry. He's a student of human nature. The Krays and Al Capone couldn't hold a candle to him.'

Harry drank some champagne. 'I'll take that as a compliment, you little Irish so-and-so. As you said, the bastard can't be touched here or apparently anywhere else, but you, with the Colonel and Billy behind you, screwed up Rashid's plans and killed his brother. Now, it's just like Brixton in the old days. Eyes everywhere. We go into Hazar to have dinner at this Excelsior place and he'll know in ten minutes.'

Professor Hal Stone said, 'Correction. Five minutes.'

'Sure,' Dillon said. 'Just like Belfast on a bad Saturday night.'

Ferguson said, 'So what do we do?'

It was Billy who answered, 'Well, actually, I'm hungry myself. I say let's go ashore to the Excelsior and take them on. If they're not there, we have a decent meal.'

Villiers laughed out loud. 'You young bastard. It's marvellous to find you confirm everything I've heard.'

'Only one thing,' Harry Salter said. 'If we go, we go tooled up.' He turned to Hal Stone. 'You know what that means, Professor?'

'I used to work for the Security Services, remember? You mean a pistol under my arm? I'm quite happy with that.'

Dillon laughed. 'If only they knew about you at high table at Corpus Christi.'

'I put up with it,' Hal Stone said. 'The wine list is excellent.'

Ferguson said, 'So we're going to eat and we're all going armed?'

'You old bugger,' Dillon said. 'You'll be disappointed if they're not there.'

*   *   *

They sat on the terrace at the Excelsior, the awning flapping, a light rain drumming. There were Ferguson, Dillon, Billy and his uncle. Hal Stone had decided to stay to watch things on the *Sultan*. There were lights on ships across the harbour, lights up in Hazar town.

'Looks like a TV programme about package holidays,' Billy said.

It was at that moment that Paul Rashid walked in with his sister.

Dillon stood up. 'Kate, you're looking grand.'

'Dillon,' she said.

Paul Rashid wore a tropical linen suit and a Guards tie.

Villiers stood up. 'Paul.' He offered his hand.

Rashid took it. 'Colonel Tony Villiers, Kate. You know the story. The Gulf War.'

Villiers turned on his considerable charm. 'Guardsmen are all the same, Lady Kate. You see the tie and always ask which regiment.'

'And you and the Earl and General Ferguson were all Grenadiers,' Dillon said.

'And Cornet Bronsby,' Billy put in. 'Let's not forget him. The Household Cavalry, Blues and Royals.'

There was a pause. It was Rashid who said, 'So I believe.'

Tony Villiers said, 'The trouble with the House-holds is that all that people see are those glamorous uniforms. They don't see them in places like Kosovo, in Challenger tanks and armoured cars.'

'They also provide a lot of volunteers for G Squadron in Twenty-Two SAS,' Ferguson put in.

'Well, that's a bleeding show stopper,' Harry said. 'I'm Harry Salter. Can I get you a drink?'

'I've heard about you, Mr Salter. You used to know the Kray brothers,' Kate said.

'They were gangsters, love, and so was I. It was what we were, only I got smart and turned legitimate.'

'Almost,' Billy said.

'Okay, almost. Glass of champagne, love?'

'No. With all due respect, there *is* a limit,' Paul Rashid told him. He turned to Dillon. 'I saw you, I knew it was you. With George, I mean.'

'And Bronsby, that means nothing?'

'George meant more.'

'The Arab side rising to the surface.'

'You couldn't be more wrong, Dillon. The Dauncey side.'

It was Ferguson who said, 'I'll be formal, my Lord. Leave it. It's gone too far. I would hope you have no expectations.'

'Of course he has,' Dillon said. 'That's why Aidan Bell isn't here.'

'Really?' Ferguson turned to Rashid. 'Could that be true?'

'Wait and see.'

'I've spoken to the Prime Minister about you. He was very angry.'

'And so was the President,' Blake Johnson said.

'What a pity.' Rashid smiled, a smile that could chill the heart. 'And I so much wanted to please the both of them. Well, I will just have to think of some other way. Good night, gentlemen.' Paul Rashid walked out, his sister on his arm.

There was silence and it was Harry Salter who said, 'I just hope you've got the message. We're going to get fucked when we leave here.'

'Really?' Ferguson opened a menu. 'Well, the kebabs they mention sound delicious. We might as well eat and enjoy ourselves.'

'And then walk down the dark streets of Hazar shoulder to shoulder?' Blake said.

'Yes, something like that, so make your choice,' Ferguson told him.

*   *   *

The Rashid Gulfstream took off from Haman and Aidan Bell sat back, accepted a whiskey and started to read a supply of English papers which had come out from London on the trip in.

The Premier and the Prime Minister were going to take a trip down the Thames to the Millennium Dome. The two-page article in the *Daily Telegraph* carried an itinerary. A night trip down the river. The major television companies would be involved and the two leaders, everything you could want.

Bell sat back, a half-smile on his face. It was like *Time* magazine and Cazalet all over again, not that Nantucket had worked out as expected, but this could be different. He'd always done well in London. All right, he'd lost the team, but this could be one of those jobs where you were better on your own.

He called to the steward for another drink and started to work through the article again.

Ferguson was right. The kebabs were excellent, and they ate with enthusiasm.

Billy said, 'All right, so we survive, which I certainly intend, we survive and get back to Wapping in one piece. What happens then, General? What's Rashid's next move?'

'Dillon?'

Dillon sat back. 'It has to have something to do with Bell. That's why he isn't here.'

'Seen getting onto a Rashid Gulfstream at Haman military airbase, booked for London,' Villiers said.

'Nice of you to tell us.'

'I decided to save it in case you didn't want dessert.'

Blake said, 'Come on, Sean, what is his agenda?'

Dillon lit a cigarette. 'He failed with the American President. He failed with the Elders. Maybe this time his target really is the obvious one. The Russian Premier's due soon in London, isn't he, Charles?'

Ferguson said, 'Come on, even he wouldn't try that now. With all the new security? Impossible.'

'You think so?' Blake shook his head. 'It should have been impossible to get as close as Bell got to the President on Nantucket. With the greatest respect to my fine Irish friend Sean Dillon here, if I gave him the job, he'd find a way. People like him always do.'

'Thank you. I love you, too,' Dillon said. 'But

he's right. Rashid would go for the Premier without a second thought.'

'And that's where Bell comes in?' Harry Salter asked.

'Well, the other year, we had the President in London. Two people, Loyalist terrorists, a man and a woman, tried to knock him off. I managed to stop them, with some assistance, and I still bear the scars.'

'What's your point?' Blake said.

'That, to use an English underworld phrase Harry and Billy know well, you don't need to go in team-handed. One person is enough, two at the most.'

'And that's true,' Billy said.

'Yes, but we're talking as if Rashid had this agenda,' Ferguson told them. 'Maybe he's had enough.'

'General,' Sean Dillon said, 'if you think that, you'll believe anything.'

'All right,' Ferguson said. 'Coffee, then let's go.'

'Tea,' Dillon said. 'I'm Irish. It goes with the rain, General.'

From the Gulfstream, Bell called Rashid on his coded mobile and caught him at the villa.

'Listen, I've had a thought.'

'Tell me.'

Bell went through the article in the *Telegraph*. 'There's a real opportunity here.'

'All right, but not the Prime Minister,' Rashid said. 'Just the Premier. The minute you're in London, go into the situation. I'll be over in a day or two anyway. I'll send instructions to give you any support you need.'

'And Dillon and company?'

'Well, I'm hoping they'll be distant history after tonight.' Bell laughed. Rashid said, 'You find this amusing?'

'Only the idea of Sean Dillon being distant history. If he's on your case, he's your worst nightmare. Having said that, I'll get on with it.'

On board the *Sultan*, Hal Stone stood in the stern, drinking a glass of cold beer, and Ali hovered. It was raining again, a fine spray, and Stone was enjoying it. He'd have to go soon, of course, back to Cambridge and students instead of being here and what he was involved with.

There was a splash in the water as Ali poured him another beer, and as Stone turned, a man pulled himself over the rail, a knife between his teeth. Ali cried out, *'Sahb!'*

Hal Stone saw, and in the same moment reached for the Browning under his left arm. He pulled it out and as the man took his knife from between his teeth shot him so that he went back over the rail. Another appeared. Stone fired again, but the Browning jammed. He grabbed Ali by the shoulder. 'The cabin. Come on.' Then he pulled him away.

Inside, he slammed and locked the door, then unloaded the Browning and took out the clip. As he discharged his bullets, someone started to kick the door in.

Dillon and the others walked down through Hazar, ready for anything and finding nothing. They reached the harbour, found the motor launch, got in and cast off, making for the *Sultan*. They coasted in.

The stern light was on under the awning, and it was quiet as Billy climbed up the ladder to tie up. Harry followed him, then Ferguson, Blake and Dillon.

At that instant, Hal Stone managed to reload the Browning and fired through the cabin door. The next moment, four Arabs ran out of the darkness to attack Ferguson's party.

Dillon fired at one of them, but the man, in a drug-crazed frenzy, rammed into him and drove him over the rail. Dillon took a deep breath, went under the *Sultan* and surfaced on the other side.

There were a couple of shots. He pulled himself up the ladder, moved in behind a crouching Arab with a knife in one hand, took his neck and twisted. There was a crack and the man slumped.

Silence. Someone said in Arabic, 'Hamid, are you there?'

'Of course,' Dillon answered and stepped forward.

He took the man, broke his right arm so that the Arab dropped the pistol and put him over the rail. It was quiet. Dillon said, 'It's me. Are you all there?'

Ferguson called, 'On the deck, but in one piece.'

Dillon said, 'Let's check if the Professor is all right, then I'd suggest we get out of this sodding place.'

'An excellent idea,' Ferguson called.

Later, Rashid came into the living room at the villa and said to Kate, 'No go. The attack on the boat failed. Ferguson, Dillon and the others have just left for London.'

'So what do we do now?' Kate Rashid asked.

'Go home, my darling . . . and try again,' her brother said.

LONDON

THE THAMES

12

In London, Bell spent time travelling up and down the Thames, following the itinerary for the Russian Premier as laid out by the *Daily Telegraph*.

He went on a trip to the Millennium Dome, then returned to the Savoy Pier. He thought about it and did the same trip the following day. There was another article discussing the visit, this time in the *Daily Mail*. He read it meticulously, noted that the riverboat for the trip was called *Prince Regent*, and that the catering was in the hands of the Orsini brothers.

He sat by the fireplace in the drawing room on South Audley Street and a plan began to form in his mind.

Rashid and Kate left in the second plane after he had made various deals with his people in the

Empty Quarter. What he was leaving was a situation so difficult that neither the Council of Elders nor the Americans, nor the Russians, would be able to handle it themselves. He also arranged for the retrieval of George's body and its return to England.

In London, Dillon went to check on Hannah. She was sitting up in bed, and by chance Bellamy was there, checking her over. Dillon excused himself and waited outside. Finally, the Professor came out.

'How is she?' Dillon asked.

'Better. It's still a wait-and-see situation as to how much back to normal she'll be. On the other hand, I remember when Norah Bell stabbed you in the back. You made it through.'

'I know. On a good day, you're a genius.'

Bellamy sighed. 'How many times have I saved your hide, Sean? I can't always succeed. Try and take care.'

He went out and Dillon thought about it, then knocked on Hannah Bernstein's door. 'How are you?'

'Pretty rotten. But I've only got to look at you

to see it's been pretty rotten for you, too. Tell me about it.'

He opened the window, lit a cigarette and sat beside her as he talked. When he was finished, she said, 'Young Billy's turning out to be a star.'

'You could say that. Bellamy says you'll make it.'

'So does my father, though I may not be able to run around Hyde Park again in the morning.'

'Well, you can't have everything.'

'As to Rashid, you might want to take a look at the papers. I read a lot of them every day out of boredom. Look at the pile over there. You should find a *Daily Telegraph*. I'd say it might interest you.' He read it and sat there thinking. 'It could fit,' she said.

'I'd say so. Do you remember the Norah Bell affair?'

'How could I forget? I shot her dead.'

'She and her boyfriend found it no problem to join the crew of that riverboat . . .'

'Waiters,' Hannah said. 'It's easy enough to carry the canapés around.'

Dillon stood up suddenly. 'I'd better go. God bless, Hannah.'

'Take care, Dillon.'

He got a cab to Cavendish Place and found Ferguson and Blake sitting on either side of the fire, talking. He explained what he had found.

'Are you suggesting the same script as with Norah Bell?' Ferguson asked.

'Hannah thinks so, and so do I. What do we do? Inform the Security Services?'

Ferguson snorted. 'That bunch? They'd only screw it up royally. You know that, Dillon.'

'All right, so what *do* we do?'

'Tell you what,' Blake said. 'I love rivers. Take me on the same trip tomorrow, Sean, and let's see what we can see.'

The next morning was typical London, the rain drifting down as Dillon and Blake boarded the *Prince Regent* at the Savoy Pier. A grey morning out of season, there were no more than fifteen people on the boat.

'It's a great city,' Blake said, as they stood under the awning at the stern. 'Even in the rain.'

'Dublin's not bad, and Manhattan has a feel to it, but, yes, the Thames is special.'

'Tell me about this business with Norah Bell, Sean.'

'An Iranian fundamentalist group called the Army of God didn't like Arafat's deal with Israel over the new status of Palestine. They also didn't care for the President presiding over the meeting at the White House and giving the agreement his blessing. So they approached a Loyalist hit man from Ulster and his girlfriend, names of Michael Ahern and Norah Bell, characters so bad that even the Red Hand of Ulster had thrown them out.'

'And what was the deal?'

'Five million sterling to kill the President.'

'My God, even I never heard of that,' Blake said.

'Oh, it was kept under wraps. The Prime Minister cooked up an evening of frivolity and cocktails for the President, cruising the Thames past the Houses of Parliament and ending up at Westminster Pier. Ahern and Norah got on board by pretending to be waiters. A confederate had left a couple of Walthers for them.'

'And?'

'Well, I managed to work it out and at the last moment joined the boat with Charles and Hannah. I killed Ahern, but Norah gutted me with a spring knife. Hannah shot her dead.' Dillon lit a cigarette. 'It was a bad scene. For a while, it looked as if I was finished, but with the help of friends, I made it.'

'A hell of a story.'

The door opened behind them and a waitress came through. 'Coffee, gentlemen, or the bar is open?'

'Coffee for me,' Blake said.

Dillon smiled. 'I'll have tea and an Irish whiskey or Scotch, if you insist.'

They stayed under the awning and the young woman finally came back with a tray.

Dillon said to her, 'So, you must be pretty excited about this big event coming up.'

'Oh, yes,' she said. 'In fact, you're lucky. Today's our last day before the company pulls the *Prince Regent* out of service to titivate it up for the big night.'

'Will you be working?' Dillon asked.

'I'm afraid not.' She was obviously disgruntled. 'Believe it or not, they're bringing in a Royal Navy crew to run the boat and some firm to do the catering. We can't even get near the place.'

'That's a hell of a shame,' Blake said.

'Yeah, but that's life. Excuse me, gentlemen.'

Blake drank his coffee and Dillon poured his whiskey into his tea as the rain increased in force.

The American said, 'What do you think?'

Dillon sighed. 'There's just something . . . I can't

put my finger on it. It's just – look, I did my time on jobs like this, right? And I never liked my left hand to know what my right hand was doing. You tried to get people to look one way so they'd miss what's happening the other way. This – it's all just flat in our face.'

'I agree, but you can't afford to take the risk, Dillon. You've got to get the security people out here in full force. All your efforts have got to be focused on this boat.'

Dillon turned, smiling, his personality almost changing. 'Jesus, son, you're right. All our efforts. It's so obvious, it's too obvious. What was I thinking?'

He pulled out his phone and got through to Ferguson. 'Blake and I are on the *Prince Regent*.'

'So you think that's where they'll hit?'

'Nope. Not in a thousand years. Have you got the itinerary there?'

'Yes.'

'Where's the Premier staying?'

'At the Dorchester, that suite on the top floor.'

Dillon said, 'Perfect. I'll get back to you.' He turned to Blake. 'He's staying on the top floor of the Dorchester. I know that suite. It's got the best rooftop views in London from its terrace. You stand out there and you can see everyone – and everyone can see you.'

'You think that's it?'

'I could be totally wrong, but if I wanted my left hand not to know what my right was doing – that's where I'd do it.'

In the drawing room at South Audley Street, Paul, Kate and Michael sat at a table with Bell. It was the moment Aidan Bell disclosed the truth.

'Ferguson's going to be on tenterhooks. He's expecting a hit, and by now he's convinced himself it'll be on the boat trip. But it won't.'

'What? Then what's your plan?' Kate asked.

'The Premier's staying on the top floor of the Dorchester. There are some lovely flat roofs below, with perfect lines of fire. I'll climb up there and do it myself.'

There was silence. Michael said, 'I'll go with you.'

'Hey, that's not necessary.'

'Bell, this time I want to make sure. I was trained as a marksman myself. I'm going with you.'

Paul Rashid said, 'And so am I.'

Kate said, 'For God's sake, Paul, what are you

thinking of? Three people? It's much too dangerous.'

'I don't care. This is our last chance, Kate. If we fail this time, then it doesn't matter if we get caught anyway.' He turned and smiled, and for the first time she thought it the smile of the truly mad. 'This is for George, Kate, and for our mother. There's no turning back.'

Dillon, Blake and Ferguson visited the Dorchester and were shown up to the suite. The views from the terrace were as advertised. They were extraordinary – and extraordinarily dangerous.

'Dillon's right,' Ferguson said. 'The Premier can't stay here.'

'How will you handle it?' Blake asked.

'No need to make a big fuss. I'll just tell the Prime Minister's office that I'm not happy with the overall security.'

'Which means you won't need to explain the plot,' Blake said.

'Exactly. Low key, that's how we'll keep it. I'll see the Prime Minister again.'

*　　*　　*

At Downing Street, Dillon sat in the Daimler while Ferguson and Blake were taken to the Prime Minister's study. He was sitting with a small man in his early fifties, with white hair and the look of the academic he'd once been. He was Simon Carter, the Deputy Director of the Security Services, and no friend of Ferguson.

'So what happened in Hazar?' the Prime Minister asked.

'Well, for one thing, the Council of Elders is still intact, thanks to Dillon.'

'Not that little Irish swine again,' Carter said.

'Carter, we're not friends, but I've never disputed your efficiency in the past. Let me tell you what Dillon achieved, if you'll allow me, Prime Minister.'

'Of course.'

Afterwards, the Prime Minister said, 'Extraordinary,' and even Carter had to agree.

'Now tell him about Nantucket,' the Prime Minister said.

This time, when Ferguson had finished, Carter said, 'It's incredible, the whole damn business.' He looked more shaken than Ferguson had ever seen him. 'Well, it's clear we'll have to cancel everything with the Premier, wipe it all out.'

'Hold on,' Ferguson said. 'We have a better idea.'

'What is that?' the Prime Minister said.

'Russian security must be told we might have a problem. I would handle it this way, if the Deputy Director approves. Allow the arrangements at the Dorchester to go through. That would be for the media.'

'And then?'

'Cancel the cocktail party on the *Prince Regent*, but only at the last moment. Any excuse will do. Change the dinner venue to somewhere like the Reform Club. I'm sure they'd love to have you, sir.'

The Prime Minister smiled. 'I'm certain of it.'

Carter said, 'And then?'

'The Premier is taken back, not to the Dorchester but to his Embassy.'

'But what would the final point be?' the Prime Minister said.

'That I would wait in the suite at the Dorchester with people of my choosing.'

'Dillon?'

'Yes, sir, and some friends of his. They did great service in Hazar. However, you wouldn't put them on the New Year's Honours List.'

'And they'd wait to see if Rashid or this man Bell turned up?'

'Yes, sir, but it's even better than that. I think the Deputy Director already sees what I'm getting at.'

Carter smiled. 'Yes.' And he turned to the Prime Minister. 'There's been no indictable proof against Rashid up to now. But if he comes, or one of his men, and we get him alive, he won't be untouchable any more. He must be getting desperate by now. At last, we can lay a trap for *him* instead of the other way around.'

'Then so be it.' The Prime Minister stood. 'It's in your hands, gentlemen. Mr Johnson, I'll speak to the President.'

Outside, it was cold. Dillon stood beside the Daimler smoking a cigarette as Ferguson, Blake and Carter approached.

Ferguson said to Carter, 'Can I give you a lift?'

'No, I feel like a walk, and sitting in the car with someone who once mortar-bombed Downing Street is more than I can take.'

Dillon said, 'Jesus, sir, the grand man you are, and absolutely right.'

In spite of himself, Carter laughed. 'Damn you, Dillon.' He moved away toward the Downing

Street gates, paused and turned back, and he wasn't smiling. 'I don't care who he is, I don't care about his medals or his money. Stop him, Dillon.'

He walked away.

Ferguson phoned Rashid at the company offices and found he was not available. A secretary asked him to wait, and after a moment, Kate Rashid came to the phone.

'General Ferguson. What can I do for you?'

'I'll be in the Piano Bar at the Dorchester at eight o'clock.'

'Am I supposed to be interested?'

'I'd earnestly advise it, Lady Kate. Bring the Earl.'

He put down the phone.

She reported to Paul, who was down at the Dauncey Arms with Bell and Michael, and told him of her conversation with Ferguson. 'I'll handle it, if you want me to,' she said.

'No,' Paul said. 'We'll come up this afternoon. I'm not going to leave you on your own with Dillon and Ferguson. Never underestimate the General. I'll see you later.'

He switched off his phone. Michael said, 'Trouble?'

'Ferguson wants a meeting. We'll go back.'

'All of us?'

'Oh, yes.' He turned to Bell. 'You'll have to keep your head down.' He smiled at Betty Moody. 'We're heading out, love.'

As they sat in the Rolls-Royce, the glass divider closed, the Earl said to Bell, 'I think you'd better not stay at the South Audley house.'

'Where would you suggest?'

'Michael has a motor cruiser parked at a place called Hangman's Wharf at Wapping. You can stay there overnight.'

'That sounds good to me.'

'This meeting, brother,' Michael asked. 'What does Ferguson want?'

'Whatever Dillon wants. We'll see.' Paul Rashid closed his eyes and leaned back.

But in London, Dillon had been doing some thinking himself. He had hooked up to Ferguson's computer and trawled the list of the Rashid company's assets. Then he called Harry Salter at the Dark Man.

'Harry. Michael Rashid has this boat parked at Hangman's Wharf in Wapping. You know everything that's going on along the river. What's the story?'

'Let me check my computer.' After a while, Salter came back, laughing. 'It's called *Hazar*.'

'Well, that fits. Is Billy there?'

'Yes.'

'Put us on conference.'

After explaining the situation, Dillon said, 'So he must have Bell tucked up somewhere. What do you think? South Audley Street or Hangman's Wharf?'

'Could be either,' Billy said. 'I'll check out South Audley for an hour or two this evening. If there's no result, I'll try the *Hazar*.'

That evening, Kate Rashid arrived first, to find Dillon waiting for her.

'What? No piano this evening, Dillon? I'm disappointed. I came all this way just to hear you play. You'd never know that your true vocation is for killing people.'

'But not torture, Kate. Not killing a young, decent man in the most horrific way. Bronsby deserved better.'

273

'Well, fuck you, too,' she said.

'Jesus, girl, did they tell you that at Oxford?'

In spite of herself, she showed a glimmer of a smile. 'Oh, posh girls can be worse than the tarts.'

'How exciting.'

He lit a cigarette, and she reached and took it from his mouth and smoked it for a moment. 'You killed my brother.'

'Who'd arranged for Bronsby to be skinned, and you and the Earl were there. Do you mean to tell me you approve of one and hate the other?'

She took a deep breath. 'Not really. I just hate you for George's death.'

'No, Kate, no, you don't. That's the problem.'

Billy and his uncle sat in a Shogun in South Audley Street, Billy at the wheel, Harry reading the *Evening Standard*. He happened to glance up and saw a Mini emerge from a side entrance to the house.

'It's Bell and Michael Rashid, Billy. Get moving.'

Paul Rashid appeared in the Piano Bar just as Ferguson and Johnson walked in. He looked well, tanned from the Hazar sun, in a cream linen suit and the usual Guards tie.

'General Ferguson.' He didn't shake hands. 'Dillon. Mr Johnson.'

They all sat down.

Ferguson said, 'It's over.'

'What is?' Rashid asked.

'You know very well. I thought I'd give you one last chance: Stop it now. You've got away with a great deal, but not again, I can promise you.'

Paul spoke softly and deliberately. 'I'm a great believer in family. I had a brother, a greatly loved brother, killed in Hazar.'

'If you'll excuse me, My Lord,' Dillon said. 'The fact that you can make such a fuss about that after what you did to Bronsby indicates that you're seriously disturbed.' Kate tossed her glass of champagne in his face. Dillon ran his tongue over his lips and reached for a napkin. 'What a waste.'

Just then, his mobile rang. 'Excuse me.' He got up and walked away. 'Dillon.'

Billy said, 'Harry and I have followed Michael Rashid and Aidan Bell to Hangman's Wharf. They've boarded the *Hazar*. Do you want to tell Ferguson?'

'No, this is our business. I didn't want Ferguson

to know, in case he says don't do it. I'll be with you in half an hour.'

He returned to the table. 'Sorry, I've got to go. I'm sure you'll handle things here, General. Tell them we know about their plans for the boat trip, and they'll never get away with it. They've come to the end of the line.'

'Do you need me?' Blake asked.

'Not this time, old son.' He looked at Paul Rashid. 'I'd listen to the General, I really would.' Then he turned and went out. Smiling.

13

It was raining, driving in across the Thames at Hangman's Wharf, as Billy and Harry parked. Billy went round and opened the tailgate of the Shogun and produced an umbrella.

'Well, that's nice,' Harry said. 'I tell you what. It doesn't make you look like Bogart in *The Big Sleep*.'

'Yes, well, I do have a shooter in my pocket,' Billy said. 'So I suppose that's all that matters.'

On board the *Hazar*, Bell and Michael Rashid had a drink. Rashid said, 'Right, you have a quiet night. I'll be in touch tomorrow, and tomorrow night, unless things change, will be the big one.'

'Well, we'll see,' Aidan Bell told him.

Outside, a voice called, 'Hey, are you there, Rashid, and that Irish fuck with you?'

Bell and Rashid drew Brownings and approached the companionway.

Dillon had arrived fifteen minutes earlier, parked behind Billy and Harry, and joined them. He called Ferguson on his mobile.

'Where are you?' Ferguson asked, so Dillon told him. 'For God's sake. What are you playing at?'

'We still can't confirm the hit, the river or the Dorchester, so I'm taking the initiative. I'm with Billy and Harry. Bell left the Rashid house with Michael, they followed to Michael's boat at Wapping, and I've joined them.'

'Dillon, just listen to me.'

'No, I'm going to listen to me, General. I'll let you know how it goes.'

He switched off.

'He wasn't pleased?' Harry asked.

'Not really. He might be if we get a result.'

'How do we play it?' Billy asked.

Dillon took off his jacket and loosened his tie as he told them. He took out his Walther and slipped it into the waistband of his trousers at the rear.

'So you do the face-to-face, Billy, and you cover him, Harry.'

'Christ, Dillon, it's going to be cold in there.'

'Never mind that. Just watch yourself, Billy. Bell's tricky.'

'Don't worry about me. Think of yourself, Dillon. You're the one at the short end.'

'Fine. Just let me go in, then do your bit.'

Harry Salter crouched behind a bollard on the wharf. Dillon went down a ladder from the edge of the wharf and sank into the water. It was bitterly cold. He swam round to the other side of the *Hazar* and discovered, as he'd expected, a boarding ladder. It was then that Billy Salter approached the *Hazar* and called out.

'Hey, are you there, Rashid, and that Irish fuck with you?'

Bell said to Michael Rashid, 'You go to the stern, I'll take the bow, and don't screw around.'

Rashid said, 'I can hold my own.'

'Get on with it, then.'

Bell left him to go up the steps to the deck and Rashid went back through the cabins and pulled himself up the transom into the shadows of the stern.

Several things happened at the same time. Harry, behind the bollard, moved and Aidan Bell fired and hit Salter in the right shoulder. The force threw him back and Bell pulled himself over the edge of the wharf and scrambled away in the shadows.

Michael Rashid fired several times and Billy returned fire. Rashid moved back against the rail . . . and Dillon reached up and pulled on his ankles and Rashid toppled over. Dillon got an arm around the neck, took a deep breath and reached for the anchor line to pull himself under. Rashid struggled, kicking, and Dillon hung on until the struggling stopped. From the shadows, Bell watched, then faded away.

Dillon released the body and pulled himself up the ladder to the wharf. Harry was on his feet, groaning, Billy supporting him.

'Sorry, Dillon, we've lost Bell.'

'Michael Rashid is dead.' Dillon turned to Harry Salter. 'Get in the Shogun. You drive, Billy. Take us to Rosedene. I'll call Ferguson. He'll pull in Professor Henry Bellamy.'

'Dillon, I'm getting too old for this,' Harry said.

'Nonsense. We'll get Dora in to nurse you.'

As they drove away, he called Ferguson. 'You're going to need the disposal team. Yes, Michael Rashid. You'll find him in the water off Hangman's Wharf by his boat, the *Hazar*.'

'You did it yourself, I suppose.'

'Bell got away after shooting Harry in the shoulder. We're on our way to Rosedene. Get Bellamy. If he's not available, Hannah's dad. Only the best.'

'Consider it done, but Dillon, it would be nice if you talked to me sometimes.'

At Rosedene, Dillon waited with Billy. Bellamy was busy doing a bypass operation at Guy's, but Arnold Bernstein had been available.

Dillon said, 'Let's look in on Hannah.'

'Suits me,' Billy said.

She was sitting up, reading the *Evening Standard*, and looking far better than when Dillon had last seen her.

'So, the two musketeers. Bring me up to date.'

Which Dillon did.

Afterwards, she sat there brooding. Dillon said, 'What do you think?'

She was silent for a moment before she answered. 'Did anyone ever tell you the details of how Paul Rashid got his Military Cross in the Gulf War?'

'No, what about it?'

'Well, I've read the file. Villiers took twenty men behind the Iraqi lines in two Russian sand cruisers.

281

Rashid was in charge of group two. Ten men. But he made a mistake. He radioed Villiers on a clear line when it looked like there was an emergency, and the Iraqis picked it up, homed in and took out every man in his command.'

Billy said, 'Except Rashid?'

'Exactly. However, when Villiers got to where Rashid was, there was no one there. Just seven Iraqi soldiers, all dead and all emasculated.'

'And Rashid?' Dillon asked.

'Reached the Allied lines ten days later, walking on his own.'

Dillon said, 'Tony Villiers never mentioned this. Why not?'

Hannah smiled and shook her head. 'That's a comfort – even the great Sean Dillon can be naïve. Look, Rashid is an Earl. And the product of Sandhurst, the Grenadier Guards and the SAS. Now, whatever else those outfits taught you, it wasn't how to cut off your opponent's cock. So *that* we keep quiet about.'

'This is all interesting stuff, Superintendent,' Billy said, 'but what's your conclusion?'

'He *is* mad. And he believes very much in revenge, in the harshest possible terms. Dillon has killed his two brothers, so Dillon must die.' She turned. 'It's the only certainty, Sean. He would be incapable of living with himself, with you alive.'

'And Kate?' Dillon asked.

'Empathetic inclusion. To aristocratic people, family is everything, and in this case there's a double dose, with the Dauncey on one hand and Rashid on the other. Kate is aware of her heritage and looks up to him as head of the family. It couldn't be otherwise.'

Billy said, 'So even she might want to kill Dillon off?'

'I would say so.' Suddenly, she looked tired. 'I need to rest.'

The door opened and her father looked in, still wearing his operating gown. 'They told me you were here.'

Billy said, 'How is he?'

'Well, my recommendation is that at your uncle's age, he should try not to get shot. Having said that, he's not going to die on us.' He moved to his daughter. 'How are you?'

'Tired.'

'Then go to sleep.' He turned to the other two. 'Out.'

They moved, Dillon got the door open, and she called, 'Sean, take care, for God's sake. Rashid is obsessed; he must kill you. In fact, he'll challenge you. It's like being back in the desert, Sean. He wants you for himself.'

She was crying. Arnold Bernstein pushed Dillon and Billy through the door and said, 'I'll be back, my love.'

Dillon said, 'She's taking it very hard. Why? She never approved of me.'

'You're such a smart man. You must be to have got away with killing people for the last thirty years. On the other hand, if you can't see why she's crying, my little Irish friend, then you really must be stupid.'

He walked away and Billy said, 'I think he means she likes you, Dillon.'

Dillon lit a cigarette. 'Yes, I did get that impression. Let's have a cup of tea. We'll hang around and maybe they'll let you see Harry before we leave.'

They went into the reception lounge, gave one of the girls an order and sat down.

Aidan Bell made it up from the river to the High Street and caught a cab to Mayfair. He walked the last few hundred yards to the back of the South

Audley Street house, where he rang the bell at the kitchen door. It was Kate who answered. Her face dropped.

'What's wrong?'

'Everything. Is he here?'

'Yes.'

'Then lead the way.'

She suddenly looked fearful. 'Where's Michael?'

'Get on with it.'

She took him to the great drawing room, where Paul Rashid sat by the fire. He looked up.

'What are you doing back here? Where's Michael?'

'There's no easy way of telling you this. Dillon turned up at Hangman's Wharf with the Salters. I managed to shoot Harry Salter, but Dillon got your brother over the rail. The last I saw, he had an arm round his neck and was taking him under the water.'

Kate let out an agonized cry, turned and stumbled away. Rashid, his face very calm, said, 'Tell me exactly what happened.'

Dillon and Billy were drinking tea in the reception lounge when Ferguson appeared. 'How's Harry?' he asked.

'He'll survive,' Billy said. 'Pay him off with an OBE.'

Ferguson turned to Dillon. 'What in the hell were you playing at?'

'I suddenly realized we didn't have any certainty. We've been talking about the *Prince Regent* and about the Dorchester and everything *sounded* right, but we didn't *know*. So Billy and Harry followed Michael Rashid and Bell to Hangman's Wharf, where Rashid had this motor cruiser. It got a bit frantic then. Bell shot Harry and got away. I pulled young Rashid over the rail and drowned him!'

'What a bastard you are, Dillon.'

'Yes, well, it's the line of work you put me in. Has the disposal team found him?'

'No, the police have. I decided to handle it that way – an anonymous phone call, someone walking the dog on the wharf who saw the body in the water.'

'And Paul Rashid?'

'Must have heard by now.'

'And Bell?'

'God knows. I'd have thought Bell was a closed chapter. You've effectively blocked any of Rashid's aspirations as regards the Premier. If Bell has any sense, he'll be well on his way out of it.'

'That's interesting,' Billy said. 'We had a very illuminating chat with Superintendent Bernstein. I didn't know she had a psychology degree. The way she analysed it, Paul Rashid is a raving loony. He'll have to kill Dillon, because of the family pride, and his sister would probably do it for him.'

'Bell,' Dillon said. 'He's mad, too, and when it comes down to it, maybe so am I. I wouldn't bank on Bell doing a runner. He loves the game, and if Rashid decides he still needs him, there could be a lot of money in it for him.'

At Kensington Mortuary, Paul and Kate Rashid waited in a grim room painted green and white. There was an electric fire, a window over a parking lot. After a while, a male nurse came in. He looked uncertain.

'Mr Rashid?'

It was Kate who said, 'No, my brother is Earl of Loch Dhu.'

'And the deceased, Michael Rashid . . . ?'

'Also my brother.'

'Would you like to see him?'

'Yes,' Paul Rashid said tonelessly.

'There's just been an autopsy. The pathologist is

still there. You mightn't find it very pleasant. I'm thinking of the young lady.'

'That's kind of you, but it must be done.'

'The thing is, there are some gentlemen in there. A General Ferguson and two others.'

Lady Kate made an exclamation, but her brother put a hand on her arm. 'That's fine. We all know each other.'

They were led into an operating theatre: white paint, lots of stainless steel. The forensic pathologist stood with Ferguson, Dillon and Blake. The nurse went and whispered to him. The pathologist turned.

'Lord Loch Dhu, I'm very sorry.'

Rashid said, 'Ferguson, if you'd be kind enough to wait outside, I'd appreciate a word.'

'Of course,' Ferguson replied, very formal, very English upper class.

He walked out with Dillon and Blake. Kate walked to the operating table where Michael Rashid lay naked, crude stitching on the body and a line around his skull.

'Was this necessary?'

'Your brother drowned, after falling over the rail of his boat, but the coroner demands a full autopsy. There's no way around that. I've established the cause of death as drowning, and under Section Three of the act, I can issue a certificate releasing the body to you. There's no need for a court hearing.'

'That's extremely kind,' Paul Rashid said. 'I'll make the necessary arrangements.'

When he and Kate went out, Ferguson was in the reception area talking to a middle-aged man in a raincoat and old-fashioned trilby hat.

The General nodded to the Rashids. 'I'll see you outside.'

The man in the trilby said, 'I'm Chief Inspector Temple. There's no evidence of foul play. Just a tragic accident.'

'Of course.'

'I presume the pathologist has told you that in these circumstances, under Section Three, he can release the body without a Coroner's Court hearing?'

'Yes.'

'I have to countersign it as investigating officer, so I'll do that now. After that, you'll be able to have the body at any time.'

There was a look in his eye, and after all, why should a Chief Inspector be the investigating officer in a drowning?

Paul Rashid smiled and took his hand. 'You've been very kind.'

Outside, Ferguson waited on the pavement beside the Daimler, his chauffeur at the wheel. Dillon stood close by with Blake, smoking.

Ferguson said, 'I don't know about you chaps, but I'm famished. There's that nice Italian restaurant next to the Dorchester, you know the one?' He turned. 'Ah, there you are.'

'My brother George's body was delivered earlier from Hazar. They're releasing Michael. We'll bury them at Dauncey in the family mausoleum the day after tomorrow. After that, it's open season.'

'Your brother drowned,' Ferguson told him. 'It's as simple as that.'

Kate walked up to Dillon and struck him in the face. 'And you drowned him.'

'Jesus, Kate, he was trying to kill me. Why is it the Rashids seem to think it's okay for them to shoot other people but not to get stiffed in return?'

She turned away and got behind the wheel of the Mercedes. Paul Rashid said, 'Vengeance is mine, Dillon. You should understand that. It's the Old Testament.'

'Well, I'll tell you what, My Lord, I'll make you

a fair offer. Being just as mad as you, I'll come to the funerals. That way, you can try to finish me off, if you can – or I might just try the same with you. What do you say to that?'

Rashid's eyes gleamed for a moment and he almost seemed to smile. Then, with a brief nod, he said, 'I'll be expecting you,' and drove off.

'Jesus,' Ferguson said. 'That was really pushing it.'

Dillon turned to him. 'It's time this whole thing ended, General.' He stared after the departing car. 'One way or another.'

As Kate drove, her brother called the number of a service flat around the corner from the South Audley Street house. Normally, it was for the use of extra staff. At the moment, it housed Bell.

When he answered, Rashid said, 'It's me. Now listen.'

He told Bell exactly what had happened. When he was finished, Bell said, 'What a bastard Sean is, but then that's how he's lived so long.'

'You talk as if you admire him.'

'He's a decent enough stick. We've a lot in common.'

'Well, I'd like to take care of this myself, but if you can do it, so be it. The three of them are on their way to some Italian restaurant next to the Dorchester. Ferguson's car is a Daimler, you can't miss it.'

'What do you want me to do?'

'Take them out. Come round to South Audley Street. I'll supply a weapon. I'll pay you, of course.'

'You're on. See you soon.'

Rashid switched off his phone. Kate said, 'You mean it?'

'Kate, I told them when the funeral would be, and I got the reaction I wanted from Dillon. So the last thing they expect is a hit now.' He shrugged. 'This is right up Bell's alley. I'll give him one more chance. If he fails this time, then I'll kill Dillon myself. After I kill Bell.'

He was so calm, so certain, there was no way she could argue and she continued to drive.

Bell arrived at the back door at South Audley Street and was let in by Rashid, who took him upstairs and unlocked a door into what proved to be a gun room. Most things were on offer, but Bell chose an Armalite.

'An old friend, this one. A folding stock, and you have a silencer.'

'It's not completely silent. What would you want to do?'

'Shoot a tyre out, get all of them at the same time.'

'That sounds good. Let's see if you can do it. Whatever happens, return to the flat. I'll expect to find you there.'

'Good. Now find me some sort of road map.'

Bell found an old raincoat with capacious pockets so that the Armalite, with its folding stock, was easily concealed. He walked down South Audley Street until he found the restaurant, and there was the parked Daimler, the chauffeur sitting with the light on, reading a newspaper.

He had worked out from the map that, on leaving the restaurant, they would have to turn left down Park Lane, then make a U-turn into Curzon Gate to make for Cavendish Place along the other side of Park Lane. So, Bell crossed the road to the shadows of Hyde Park, scrambled over the fence and stood in the darkness of a tree. He had a pair of night glasses, which he clipped to his head, and he watched the front of the restaurant.

When Ferguson, Blake and Dillon emerged, they walked to the Daimler and got in. Bell took out the Armalite, unfolded it and waited. There was little traffic at that time of night and the Daimler turned out of Curzon Gate and picked up speed. Bell aimed at the rear wheel on the passenger side and fired. At that moment, Dillon happened to turn his head and saw the flash. The tyre burst and the Daimler slewed across the road, then back again, bumping over the kerb. Ferguson was thrown against the passenger door, Blake on his knees.

'This is a hit,' Dillon said, 'I saw the flash. I'm going.'

He jumped out, vaulted the fence and drew his Walther. Aidan Bell turned and ran, holding the Armalite across his chest.

Dillon went after him, chasing him through the shadows. They came to a huge monument, suffused with light all around, and Bell tripped and fell, and the Armalite went flying. Dillon came to a halt and stood there, chest heaving, holding the Walther to his side.

'Why, Aidan, it's you, old son. How much did the Earl offer?'

'To hell with you, Dillon.'

He grabbed for the Armalite and Dillon shot him twice in the heart.

He went back to the road and the car. Ferguson was holding his arm. 'I think it's broken.'

'What happened, Sean?' Blake asked.

'It was Bell. I shot him. He's by the monument. I don't know how you want to handle it, General. Do you want to leave a famous IRA terrorist to be found shot dead in Hyde Park or call in the disposal team?'

'In the circumstances, let's make it low-key. You call in, explain where you are and wait. Frankly, I need to get myself to Rosedene.' He got out of the Daimler with Blake and said to his chauffeur, 'Call in recovery for the car. Mr Johnson will see to me.'

Later, sitting in the shadows of the monument, Dillon rang Paul Rashid on his mobile. 'It's me, Dillon. Aidan Bell tried to take us out, but I'm afraid he's failed for the very last time.'

'You've killed him?'

'Yes.'

'Well, if you hadn't done it, I would have.'

'That doesn't surprise me. I'm looking forward to the funeral, Rashid. If you think you can take me, you're welcome to do it. This thing's gone on long enough.'

'I look forward to it as well, Dillon.'

Kate, sitting opposite him, said, 'What is it?'

'Bell's dead.'

'Dillon?'

'Who else.'

'So, he'll come to the funeral?'

'He'll come to his death as far as I'm concerned.'

Dillon sat on the steps of the monument, smoking a cigarette, and after a while, the disposal team arrived.

DAUNCEY PLACE

14

Blake went home the following morning. Bell vanished off the face of the earth. Dillon visited Rosedene and found Ferguson with his left arm in a sling by Hannah's bed.

'How are you?' Dillon asked.

'I've been better.'

Dillon turned to Hannah. 'And you?'

'I'll survive. General Ferguson has filled me in. So, you killed Bell?'

'You sound disapproving. For God's sake, woman, he tried to kill us.' He smiled. 'Ah, I see it now. You're not in favour of capital punishment.'

'Damn you, Dillon. The General says you told Rashid you'd attend the funerals of his brothers tomorrow.'

'So? You told me he'd challenge me. I figured I'd just challenge him first.'

'You stupid man. I told you, he's crazy. He'll do anything to finish you off now.'

'And as I've told you many times, Hannah, I just may be crazy, too.'

'I really don't think you should do it, Dillon,' Ferguson said. 'In fact, that's an order.'

Dillon said, 'And if I say no, what will you do, lock me up in Wandsworth Prison?'

'I could. Your past record condemns you.'

'Really? When you got me out of a Serbian prison, blackmailed me to come and be your enforcer, the important part of the deal was that my IRA slate would be wiped clean. Now, in effect, you tell me no. If you're serious, all I can say is that Billy Salter may be a gangster, but he's got a grip on morality that's far better than yours.' He reached over and kissed Hannah on the cheek. 'God bless, girl, and take care. As for Rashid wanting me dead, well, the British Army wanted that for long enough and I'm still here.' He nodded to Ferguson. 'You know where to get me if that's what you want to do. Otherwise I'll go down to Dauncey tomorrow to that funeral. I'll give Rashid his chance.'

He turned and went out.

Hannah said, 'Are you going to have him banged up, sir?'

'Of course not.' Ferguson sighed. 'I just wanted to see if I could bluff him out of it. These past eight or nine years, I've grown rather fond of him. You, too, I think.'

'You could say that, sir, but I'd appreciate it if you'd promise not to tell him.'

'Of course, my dear. Now, as I'm feeling perfectly wretched, I think I'll go home.'

Paul and Kate Rashid went into the Dauncey Arms at lunchtime. Betty Moody was behind the bar and all the usual locals were there. Everyone stood up.

Rashid said, 'No, my friends, sit down. Get a drink for everyone, Betty, but I'm hungry as a hunter. Whatever you've got.'

There were tears in her eyes. She reached and touched his face. 'Oh, Paul,' and then Kate was crying, too, and Betty took her hand and lifted the bar flap. 'You stop snivelling, girl. I've told you that since you first learned to listen. Come and do some useful work in the kitchen.'

Later, they ate, she opened a bottle of champagne for them and they sat by the fire.

'Tomorrow,' she said hesitantly. 'The funerals. You haven't said much.'

'Service at the church is eleven thirty. We're scaling it down this time, Betty. No general invitation like the last time. The villagers are welcome, though. You could do us a buffet here at the pub. We don't want a fuss. I don't even want staff at the house after the funeral.'

'Whatever you want, Paul, leave it with me.'

She moved away. Kate said, 'Will he come?'

'Oh, yes, he'll come,' her brother said. 'I've never been more certain of anything in my life.'

Dillon called in on Harry at the Rosedene and found him propped up in bed, Dora hovering, the epitome of the barmaid turned nurse.

'Watch it,' Dillon told her. 'If you keep doing such a good job, the old bugger might decide to marry you.'

Her eyes gleamed. Harry said, 'Don't give her ideas above her station!' He slapped Dora's bottom. 'Go and find me a bottle of Scotch, there's a good girl.'

She went out. Dillon said, 'You think you've got her, but she's got you by your bits and pieces, Harry. Mind you, you're a lucky sod. She's actually a damn nice woman and she'd kill for you.'

'You don't need to tell me.'

'Then treat her right.'

Salter looked at him. 'Why do I get the impression you're not exactly on top of the world?'

'Ah, well, we all have our ups and downs. I've seen Hannah. You know how it is. She loves me and hates me and worries about me.'

'You're going to do something stupid,' Harry said. 'Christ, Dillon, you really are going down to Dauncey to that double funeral tomorrow.'

'It's a challenge, Harry. He wants to face me. I killed his two brothers. He's entitled.'

'You know what, my old son, that sounds like a death wish to me. Are you thinking of pulling Billy in? There isn't anybody else.'

'No. I'm going to drop in at the Dark Man and have a bite to eat, but Billy's done enough. You know, Harry, he calls himself my younger brother, and in a way that's what he's become. I'm not putting him in harm's way again. I won't ask him to go to Dauncey tomorrow. For all I know, the Earl could set the dogs on us.'

'So you're going to go down there wearing a black suit and stand in the congregation at the Dauncey parish church?'

'It has to be done, Harry.'

'Well, that's nice, isn't it? Just when I was willing to accept you as Billy's older brother, you're going to put your head on the chopping block.'

Dillon got up. 'Harry, you're a diamond, and so is Billy, but there comes a time . . .'

'Yes, I know. When a man's got to do what a man's got to do. John Wayne, rest in peace.' Dora came in with a bottle of Scotch. Harry said, 'Go on, clear off, Dillon, you're making me angry.'

Dillon went. Harry sat there, absentmindedly fondling Dora's rear, then reached for the bedside phone and rang his nephew's mobile. Billy was at the Cable Wharf office.

'Listen, Dillon's just left me. He said he was going to call in and have a bite of lunch with you. As you know, Rashid's burying his brothers at Dauncey church tomorrow, and Dillon's determined to go and face up to him. Like some kind of Gunfight at the OK Corral. What's more, he's going to go on his own.'

Billy said, 'No way. If he goes, I go with him. I know you might not approve.'

'Actually, Billy, I'm proud of you, only don't tell him. Just say he's stupid. We'll let him go, then catch up later.'

'You say we?'

'Billy, even with Dora, I can't be here for ever. At least I can give you moral support. We'll follow Dillon down.'

At the Dark Man, trade was busy, with plenty of cars parked on Cable Wharf. It was raining on the river again, that season of the year. Dillon found an old umbrella in the Mini Cooper's boot, put it up, lit a cigarette and walked for a while.

He was strangely melancholy, a feeling that he was somehow at the end of things. He didn't hate Paul Rashid, and Kate, as most men would have to admit, he admired tremendously. He had killed many times over the years. It was his nature. He'd excused himself by claiming the death of his father, caught in the middle of a firefight in a Belfast Street between IRA members and British paratroopers.

But what if it really *was* his nature, his father's death only an excuse? What did that say about him? He could argue that, in his way, he'd been a soldier for years, but could he condemn Rashid and not condemn himself? The only difference between them, the thing that really was unacceptable, was Cornet Bronsby's appalling death.

He lit another cigarette, slightly morose and

depressed. 'Oh, to hell with it. What's getting into me?'

At that moment, he was hailed from the door of the pub and turned to find Billy running toward him. He ducked under the umbrella.

'What are you trying to do, drown yourself?'

'Something like that.'

'Oh, I see, a bad hair day. Let's all feel sorry for Sean Dillon.'

'Go to hell,' Dillon told him.

'Yes, well, you need some Dark Man food in you, and a drink. I mean, you're an older guy. You can't go through what we have in the last few weeks and come out of it as fresh as I do.'

Dillon laughed out loud. 'You cheeky young sod.'

'That's better.'

He led the way inside, where the bar was busy, but Baxter and Hall had the end booth. Billy and Dillon found them, and Billy said, 'Scarper, you two, we've got things to discuss. Tell the bird at the bar to bring us a bottle of Bollinger, two glasses and some Irish stew.'

The Irishman said, 'What is this, be nice to Dillon week?'

'Come off it. You killed Rashid's two brothers,

and now he wants your balls and expects you to go to Dauncey tomorrow and face up to him, Superintendent Bernstein said, and for some reason, you want to give him his chance. He's the one who's crazy.'

'And maybe me, too, Billy, like I said.'

'Bollocks. I've never known when you didn't know exactly what you're doing. You speak several languages, you can fly any kind of plane, you're a master diver. Harry told me all about it. You were the one who challenged Rashid – and now you've got this daft idea you're going to do it on your own. Well, I won't let you. I told Harry that.'

'He must have loved that.'

'Actually, he approved. He told me to let you go, then he and I would follow you down. "Moral support" was a phrase he used.'

One of the young girls behind the bar brought a bucket of ice, Bollinger and glasses. Dillon nodded to Baxter and Hall at the bar, drinking beer.

'A glass each for those two.'

'You're so considerate,' Billy said.

'I'll show you how considerate I can be. I'm actually going to give you your wish, Billy. You can walk down the street with me just like in a bad movie. I'll supply Walthers and titanium waistcoats, because he means it, Billy. Like Hannah Bernstein said, he couldn't live with me alive. He'd love getting you, too.'

'I know,' Billy said. 'But I'm going to cover your back.'

'There's only one thing, Billy. Ferguson knows I'm going and won't stop me, but Harry, as much as he may joke about it, really is getting older. I don't want him worrying about you.'

'So what do we do?'

'You phone him late tonight at the Rosedene and tell him Ferguson's had me put in the nick to stop me doing anything stupid. You and I can clear off for Dauncey in the morning. You provide the limousine. The service is at eleven thirty. Will you do it that way?'

'He'll never forgive me, but yes, I will.'

Dillon toasted him. 'Cheers, as you say in the East End, and Billy, try and make it a black suit. I will.'

'The undertaker look?'

'Exactly.'

'Terrific.' The girl brought Irish stew. 'I can't wait,' Billy said, and called Joe Baxter and Sam Hall to him. 'Joe, I need the Jaguar first thing in the morning. Dillon and I are taking a run down into the country. The Rashid place, Dauncey, so wear a chauffeur's uniform. We're going to a funeral.'

'Whatever you say, Billy.'

Billy looked up at Hall. 'You'll have to take over for me at the warehouse, handle those black-market cigarettes from Calais. Now, another thing. I don't want Harry to know, because if he does, he'll want to come, so keep shtoom. He's already taken one bullet.'

'And we don't want him to take another,' Dillon told them.

Baxter nodded. 'So I'm the kind of chauffeur with a shooter in the glove compartment?'

'Absolutely. This Rashid is bad news, you know the story, boys. Mind you, Joe, if you'd rather not . . .' Billy said.

Baxter was outraged. 'Don't insult me, Billy. We've been together since we were seventeen.'

Billy kept eating his Irish stew. 'If Harry checks on me, you say I've been called to Southampton about that booze consignment.'

Hall said, 'He'll go crackers when he finds out the truth, Billy.'

'Yes, well, he's gone crackers before. Dora will

calm him down, show him he's still a man. Now don't let me down. Go on, get something to eat.'

Dillon said, 'So we're into hard times again?'

'Absolutely.' Billy grinned. 'You've changed my life, Dillon, persuaded me I have a brain. What was I before? Four no-big-deal prison sentences, a kind of gangster of the third rank. How many people have I killed now in circumstances you've pulled me into? As we said before, a life not put to the test is not worth living. I'll con Harry about you later.'

'As he would say, you young bastard.'

'I've got a great idea. I hear that fringe theatre the Old Red Lion, is doing this Brendan Behan play about the IRA called *The Hostage*.'

'A masterpiece.'

'Great. Let's go and see it. It'll fill in the evening . . . and maybe I'll learn something about you.'

'You're on,' Dillon said.

As a performance, it was a huge success, and afterwards in the bar, they discussed and argued about the points Behan had made. Joe Baxter, who had driven them to the Old Red Lion and been forced to watch the play, sat there, bemused.

They dropped Dillon off at Stable Mews and Billy phoned Harry at Rosedene.

'I hope I haven't called too late?'

'I can't sleep, Billy. I've been in bed too long. Now what happened with Dillon? I expected you to get back to me.'

'Well, I saw him for lunch at the pub and he was full of going down there, like you said, but there was a development this evening.'

'What kind of development?'

'Well, Ferguson warned him off going down to the funeral, and when Dillon wouldn't promise to do as he was told, he had him lifted by Special Branch. Something about Dillon's record with the IRA.'

'But Ferguson had that wiped clean when Dillon agreed to work for him.'

'Yes, well, he's had him banged up.' Billy warmed to his story. 'They've got him at West End Central. At least they've got decent cells there.'

Harry Salter was outraged. 'Bloody disgraceful. Ferguson gave his word to Dillon when he got him out of that Serb prison.'

'Yes, well, he's upper class, the General,' Billy said. 'It's the class system, Harry. The country's still riddled with it.'

'And we're supposed to be the bad guys?' Harry was fuming. 'Wait till I see Ferguson again, and I thought he was a true Brit.'

'Harry, this is bad for your blood pressure. Have a decent night's sleep. I'll call in tomorrow.'

The following morning at Stable Mews, Dillon dressed carefully, as he'd told Billy, a black suit, white shirt, black tie.

'Jesus, son,' he said, looking at himself in the mirror. 'You look like you're auditioning for a part as a Mafia hit man in *Godfather Four*.' He frowned and said softly, 'Is that what it's all about, the theatre of the street? Was that it, Belfast from the very beginning, all those years?'

The doorbell rang. He went down to the hall, found an Armani duster coat in black and the weaponry bag. When he opened the door, Billy was there, black suit and tie, curiously elegant. Baxter stood against the Jaguar in uniform.

'Hey, you're looking great,' Billy said.

Dillon opened the weaponry bag and took out a titanium waistcoat. 'As you know, this thing will stop a Forty-Five at point-blank range. I've already got mine on under my shirt. Come in the cloakroom and put this one on, Billy. We'll wait.'

'If you say so.'

Billy went into the cottage and Dillon nodded to Baxter. 'Open the boot, Joe.'

Baxter obliged. Dillon put the weaponry bag and his coat in, and opened the bag. From the assortment of weapons, he produced a Browning and a silencer.

'With luck, you might not need it, Joe, but on the other hand . . .'

Baxter smiled coldly. 'Who knows?' He opened the driver's door, reached for the glove compartment and slipped the weapon inside. A moment later, Billy came out, another coat on his arm.

'I figured this was for me, Dillon.'

'It could rain,' Dillon said.

'Great. Mind you, on the other hand you could put an Uzi in one of these pockets. I like walking in the rain. It puts you in your own private world. Let's go.'

They got in the rear and Baxter drove away.

Harry sat up in bed, Dora beside him eating a boiled egg and toast fingers. He'd had a sleepless night, so it was already mid-morning. He said, 'Get me the office. I want to speak to Billy.'

She tried, then turned, phone in hand. 'Billy isn't there. It's Sam Hall.'

Harry reached for the phone. 'Where is he, Sam?'

'There was a problem with the booze consignment and he's been called to Southampton.'

'Well, he might have told me. I'll call him on his mobile.'

Hall, panicky, said, 'I just found it on his desk, Harry.'

'Stupid young bugger. Okay, if he rings in, tell him to contact me.'

Still a major in the Army Reserve, Paul Rashid was entitled to wear uniform on appropriate occasions, and as he pulled on his tunic and adjusted the Grenadier Guards buttons in front of his dressing table mirror, his medals made a brave show. He picked up his dress cap and went out.

The centre of Dauncey Place upstairs was a great circular minstrel gallery; all the main rooms led off it. A stairway went down to the Great Hall, and above, the curving staircase of the Bell Tower lifted above the old house. Paul adjusted his cap and went down the stairs and found Kate standing by the fireplace, logs burning. Betty Moody stood nearby in a black suit.

Betty came forward, reached up and kissed his cheek. 'Oh, Paul, how wonderful you look.'

'Well, it's the least I could do for the boys. One Para wanted to send an honour guard and a bugler for George, but as I told you, Kate and I want it muted this time.'

'I only came to check the final arrangements. The buffet at the pub is set up and the champagne. You do want champagne?'

'We're celebrating their lives,' Rashid told her.

'But later? You said you didn't want anyone up at the house, not even servants.'

'Kate and I will leave the buffet early after saying hello to everyone. We want to be quiet, we want to be alone.'

'Of course. I'll go now. I'll see you later.'

She went out, and the great door clanged. Kate wore a black jacket with a black jumpsuit underneath, a gold chain round her throat, and diamond earrings.

'You look very nice,' he said.

'And you look wonderful. A true hero.'

'It would be nice to think so, little sister. Shall we go?'

They took the Range Rover from the stable block, Kate driving, went down the long drive, turned to the village and parked by the green. A few vehicles were already there.

They got out and moved to the door of the Dauncey Arms, passing the parked Jaguar, Joe Baxter already beside it in his uniform. There were many people, mostly locals, in the saloon bar, and amongst them Dillon and Billy standing by the fireplace in their black suits and duster coats.

Kate gave a sharp intake of breath. 'He came.'

'Didn't you think he would?' Rashid moved through the crowd with her, grasping hands, thanking people for coming.

'Glad you could make it, Dillon.'

'A great performance,' Dillon said to him.

'Glad you approve. I love the coats. Amazing what will go in those big pockets. And very considerate of you to bring your friend here.'

'What do you want to do, pay me off for Rama? Do what you did to Bronsby?' Billy shook his head. 'Just try, that's all I ask.'

Kate said, 'Paul, let's go.'

Betty came up, frowning. 'Is there a problem?'

'Not at all. These gentlemen are friends of mine.' Rashid smiled. 'Buffet and champagne afterwards.' Betty turned away. 'And then I'll expect you at Dauncey Place, if that's your pleasure.'

'Well, it's certainly my bleeding pleasure,' Billy told him.

'Excellent. I look forward to it. Come on, Kate.' And they turned away.

People started to filter into the church from eleven o'clock. Still, only a few limousines were outside this time, unlike the old Earl's funeral and Lady Kate's. As Rashid had arranged it, the great and the good were virtually excluded although, as before, one of the most important Imams in London had agreed to appear with the Rector, a measure of the liberality of the Muslim religion not often appreciated by outsiders.

Dillon moved in, with Billy. People were seating themselves, others walking around examining the marble edifices of the long dead. Billy was walking ahead, joining in. He suddenly paused, then motioned to Dillon.

'Look at this geezer, Sir Paul Dauncey. Says he died in fifteen-ten.'

'He's the original Paul,' Dillon said. 'The one who fought for Richard III at Bosworth, a bad day for his side. He escaped to France and the new King, Henry Tudor, pardoned him.'

'How do you know all this?'

'I looked it up, Billy. It's all in *Debrett's* – that's the bible of the English aristocracy.'

Billy looked down at Sir Paul Dauncey. 'He even looks like Rashid.'

'That kind of thing happens in families, Billy.'

'I tell you what, he looks a hard bastard.'

'He looks like a warrior, Billy, which is what he was.' He shrugged. 'It's what Rashid is. To be honest, it's what you are. Remember something I once told you? There are men of a rough persuasion who look after those things ordinary people can't handle in life. Usually, they're soldiers of one kind or another.'

'Just like you and me.'

'In a manner of speaking.' Dillon smiled. 'Now let's move to the back of the church.'

The congregation settled, the organ started to play and Major Paul Rashid, Earl of Loch Dhu, and Lady Kate Rashid came through the main entrance, followed by the undertakers carrying the two coffins, one behind the other. Each was draped in the Union flag. George's had his paratrooper's red beret on top, Michael's the cap he'd worn when passing out of Sandhurst, and in both cases, the ceremonial *jambiya* of a Rashid chieftain. The Rector had moved in from the vestry, followed by the Imam.

There was silence. The Rector said, 'We are here to celebrate the lives of two young men. George and Michael are Rashids but also Daunceys, a bloodline linked to our village that has borne that name since the fifteenth century.'

The service began.

Later, it rained as the coffins were taken to the family mausoleum. The congregation followed, one undertaker carrying a huge black umbrella over Rashid and Kate. Baxter had parked the Jaguar by the churchyard gate. Billy ran down to him and came back with a brolly.

'Jesus, I've never seen so many umbrellas.'

'It's life imitating art. I could do with a cigarette and a large Bushmills, in that order.'

'So we're going to this buffet at the pub?'

'Why not? In for a penny, in for a pound.'

He turned and walked away, and Billy followed.

15

At the Jaguar, Joe Baxter got out, and Dillon said, 'We'll walk. You wait by the green, Joe.'

Baxter glanced at Billy, who said, 'What he says goes, just do it.'

'As you say, Billy.'

He got in and drove away as Dillon lit a cigarette. Billy said, 'We're not tooled up yet.'

'There's time for that, Billy, plenty of time. Let's take a walk.' And they moved down towards the green, Billy holding the umbrella over them.

In London, Harry Salter called Sam Hall but had difficulty in contacting him. A young woman secretary informed him that Sam was taking care of a consignment down the river. In truth, Sam was well and truly keeping his head down.

Harry, totally frustrated, told Dora to arrange

his car and a driver and got dressed. She had to help him because his shoulder wound needed its sling. As she finished, the matron looked in.

'Are you discharging yourself, Mr Salter?'

'No, I'm just going home. I'll come back any time you want for my check-up.'

'Well, Professor Bernstein's here at the moment, having a look at General Ferguson, but I don't think for long.'

'You mean Ferguson's here?'

'Certainly.'

'You show me where.'

A little while later, he sat in a reception area, fuming. A door opened and Ferguson emerged, followed by Arnold Bernstein, briefcase in hand.

'Why, Harry,' Ferguson said.

'Don't Harry me, you old sod.'

Bernstein said, 'I can't remember telling you you could get out of bed, Mr Salter.'

'Well, I'm out and I'm going. I'll sign anything you want, only I need a word with his Highness here.'

'Oh dear, trouble?' Bernstein sighed. 'I'm going to see my daughter. I'll be back shortly, and I urge you to seek my advice. You need the correct medication at least.'

He walked away and Harry turned on Ferguson. 'What a bastard you are, having Dillon banged up.'

Ferguson said, 'What in the hell are you talking about?'

'Billy told me last night. You had Special Branch lift him, using the old IRA record you were supposed to wipe clean, and banged him up at West End Central to stop him going to the Dauncey funerals and confronting Rashid.'

Ferguson said, 'I ordered Dillon not to go. He wouldn't listen. You say Billy told you this?'

'Yes.'

'Where is he? Phone him now.'

'Well, he's unavailable. A job in Southampton.' A look of horror appeared on his face. 'Oh, God, he lied to me. Dillon's gone down there.'

'And I think you'll find Billy has gone, too, to watch his back. It's the only likely explanation for his absence.'

'I knew he wanted to go and I said I'd go, too.'

'Well, that explains a lot. You've been damaged enough. He wanted to keep you out of it. You see, a face-to-face confrontation with Rashid will probably be like a spaghetti Western.'

'And you're letting this happen? You're worse than me.'

Ferguson said, 'Because of our connection over the last few years, I've really had you checked out. In your days of Empire as one of the most important Guvnors – I believe that's the phrase – you fought off the Corelli brothers, three of them, who totally disappeared. Then there was Jack Hedley, the one called Mad Jack. Found in an alley off Brewer Street. I could remind you of a few more.'

'All right,' Harry said. 'That was business. It was only ever that with me. I never did whores, never did drugs.'

'I know, Harry, you just killed people who got in your way. I do the same thing or have it done. There's always a good reason. It's my job, Harry, it's business.'

'So what are you getting at?'

'I've had enough of Rashid. I don't need to go into it. You know what he's been responsible for. His two brothers have gone down, thanks to Dillon. Bell and his cronies are out of it. That only leaves Rashid, and he's got to go, too.'

'But you didn't want Dillon to go down to that funeral and face Rashid's challenge.'

'So I'm a liar, Harry. I pushed Dillon a little, but I knew he'd go, and if he finishes Rashid in the right way, it suits me. You see, Dillon is a remarkable man not just because of his many gifts and his good brain and the fact that he can kill without it giving him a problem.'

'So what have you left out?'

'He couldn't care less whether he lives or dies.'

'That's good, that's very comforting, and my nephew's going the same way?'

'Your nephew was, to use London underworld parlance, a right villain. His involvement with Dillon over the past few years has given him a sense of himself. He actually has quite a brain on him.'

'All right, so I know that, but what do we do?'

Ferguson glanced at his watch. 'The funeral service started at eleven thirty. There's a buffet afterwards at the Dauncey Arms, mainly for villagers. As it's now twelve thirty, I don't think there's much we can do except rely on Dillon.'

'And Billy?'

'Of course Billy.'

Bernstein came back. 'So, you're still leaving, Mr Salter?'

'I have to,' Harry said.

'All right. Come to the reception desk and I'll

arrange the right antibiotics, but I insist on seeing both of you tomorrow at my rooms in Harley Street at ten o'clock. I'll sort you out then.'

People ate and drank champagne at the Dauncey Arms, Betty Moody supervising everything tirelessly. Dillon and Billy joined in, had some salad, smoked salmon, new potatoes. Billy, as usual, only drank water. Dillon tried the champagne and rejected it as reasonably inferior.

A young woman leaned over the bar. 'Are you Mr Dillon?'

'That's right, my love.'

'This champagne is just for you.' She held it up. 'Cristal.'

'The best,' Dillon said. 'Now who would do a thing like that?'

'Why, the Earl, sir.'

As she removed the cork, Dillon looked round the room. There was no sign of Rashid. The girl poured, offered Billy one and he waved it away.

'The Earl doesn't seem to be here.' Dillon emptied the glass in a single swallow.

The girl looked bewildered. 'That's strange, sir. He was at the fireplace with Lady Kate.'

'Did he say anything else?'

'Oh, yes, he said if you'd call in, he'd buy you the other half.'

'Well, that's nice of him.'

'Another glass, sir?'

'No, thanks. I'll have a large Bushmills whiskey. It could be my last. No water.'

She gave it to him. Betty Moody moved in from the back kitchen. Her face was swollen with weeping. Dillon raised his glass.

'A terrible day for you, Mrs Moody.'

'For all of us.'

He said, '*L'chaim*' and swallowed the Bushmills down.

'*L'chaim?* What's that?'

'A Hebrew toast. It means "to life".' He put down his glass and turned to Billy. 'We must go,' and led the way out.

Dauncey Place was quiet when Rashid and his sister went in through the massive door and entered the Great Hall. As he had arranged, there was no staff: it was theirs alone. The logs burned in the fireplace, and on the centre table was an ice bucket with a bottle of Bollinger and four glasses. He helped her off with her raincoat and moved to open the champagne bottle.

'Why four glasses?' she asked.

'Two for Dillon and Billy Salter.' He poured. 'They'll come and I'm a gracious host, both as a Rashid and a Dauncey.' He gave her a glass and raised his own. 'To us, little sister, and George and Michael, and to Dillon.'

She drank a little. 'You don't hate him.' It was a statement, not a question.

He shrugged. 'Kate, our father was a soldier and took a soldier's risks. Sean Dillon is a soldier, I am still a soldier, George took a soldier's risks in Hazar, Michael at Wapping. Each time, Dillon took the same risks.'

'You really think that?'

'Of course.' He raised his glass. 'To Sean Dillon from Paul Rashid, one brave man to another.'

She said, 'Do you want to do this, brother?'

He refilled his glass. 'My darling girl, I've done everything in my time, put my life on the line, made incredible riches, but at the end of the day how much money can you spend?'

'So what's important?'

'Oh, I suspect Dillon would say the game.'

'And that's how you see it?'

He swallowed his champagne and laughed out loud. 'Oh, yes, Kate, the only game in town.'

The fire crackled, it was very quiet. She looked around the Great Hall. 'All we have ever been as Daunceys.'

'All our yesterdays is the phrase.'

'So what happens now?'

'Dillon will come with Billy Salter.'

'And what do you do?'

'Face him, Kate, a far more interesting prospect than making another billion.'

There was a long pause, and she sighed. 'You haven't answered, Paul.'

By the champagne bucket, there were two small transceivers. He picked one up. 'These are very simple things. Press the red button and you're in touch with me.'

'But why?'

He smiled. 'I'll explain, but first you must have a final glass with me.'

'I don't like that. It's as if you're saying goodbye.'

'Never, my darling. We'll always be together, always.'

*   *   *

329

Dillon and Billy found Baxter, drove up to Dauncey Place in the Jaguar and pulled into the stable yard. They got out, Baxter opened the boot and Dillon unzipped the weaponry bag. He took out two Walthers, put one in his belt at the rear, and gave the other to Billy.

'Is this it?' Billy asked.

'No.' Dillon took out two Parker-Hales. 'Just like Rama.' He put one in the left-hand pocket of his coat.

'So how do we do it?' Billy asked.

'Unless he's brought reinforcements, he's in there with his sister, but I'd discount her.'

'How do you know?'

'Just a feeling.'

'So we knock on the front door?'

'Maybe it's open. Let's see. You come with us, Joe, and bring your Browning.'

The three of them went up the steps of the great pillared doorway. Dillon tried the ornate handle, the ring in the lion's mouth. The door opened a couple of inches and he closed it.

'Too obvious an invitation. Let's try the terrace.'

Exactly as Rashid had anticipated. They moved along the series of french windows that fronted the library. One of them stood open.

'So, he's giving us a chance.'

Inside, between ornate curtains, was a book cupboard, the kind of thing usually concealed and painted in seventeenth-century Italian style. It stood slightly open, Kate inside.

'Now what?' Billy asked.

'I'll take the front door, you go this way, only try not to shoot me by mistake.' Dillon turned to Baxter. 'You go round the back of the house. Fire the Browning in the air three times and take off the Carswell so he'll hear it.'

'And think we're coming in that way? That's crap,' Billy told him.

'I know, but it's the best I can do. Billy, it's a question of what Rashid wants to do.' He turned to Baxter. 'On your way and we'll go straight in. See you, Billy.'

'In hell,' Billy told him.

'No chance. A bottle of champagne for me and Irish stew for both of us at the Dark Man,' and Dillon moved away.

Kate, having heard everything, closed the cupboard door and signalled her brother. He responded at once. 'What's happening?' She told him. He said,

'Good. I'll draw him up to the Bell Tower, meet him on Angel Terrace. You stay out of it.'

He clicked off. Up there, on the minstrel gallery, he moved to the balustrade holding a silenced AK-47, its butt folded. He was still wearing his uniform, but no cap. He waited.

The shots rang out, Baxter ran for it, Billy pushed the window in and went through. Dillon, at the front door, turned the lion's head handle and moved in.

The hall was a place of shadows, flames from the burning logs reflected in a strange way. Dillon was behind the chairs of the enormous dining table. Rashid saw him for a moment but didn't bother to fire.

'Hey, Dillon. Why the big coat? Parker-Hale in the pocket?' Dillon crouched, the Walther in his hand. 'I can see you. Infra-red sight. I'm up here on the minstrel gallery. Take the main staircase, then what we call the Blue Arch to the circular stairway up the Bell Tower. Angel Terrace is above the leads. I'll wait for you, if you have the courage. If you need a machine pistol, okay, but a Walther's fine with me, or bare fists.'

He laughed and the library door creaked open. Billy whispered, 'You there, Dillon?'

Using his infra-red sight, Rashid targeted the chest and fired twice. Dillon recognized the distinctive muted crack of a silenced AK-47 at once. Billy was hurled back.

'One down,' Rashid called, and his laughter faded away.

Dillon crawled to Billy, who moaned, gasped for breath. Dillon tore his shirt open, felt around and found the two rounds sticking in the titanium waistcoat.

'Take your time,' he whispered. 'You've got traumatic shock to the cardiovascular system, but the vest stopped penetration. Buy shares in the Wilkinson Sword Company.'

Billy gasped, 'I'll make it.'

'Hang on until your breathing is right. I'm going up this Bell Tower after him.'

He stood, took off his coat and left it with the Parker-Hale. When he crossed the hall and went up the stairs, his only weapon was the Walther in his right hand.

Billy lay there, trying to steady his breathing. The library door behind him creaked again. Lady Kate Rashid peered down at him, then dashed across the hall and went up the great staircase after Dillon.

*   *   *

Dillon took no particular precautions going up the circular stairway of the Bell Tower. Rashid wanted him on top, wanted to face him, that was an essential part of the situation. Beside the door at the top was a slit window. He peered through. What was obviously the Angel Terrace curled away, with no sign of Rashid.

Dillon opened the door, flattened himself to one side and looked out. The rain had increased into an almost tropic downpour. There was a curved railing and on the other side, the old-fashioned roof, made of sheets of lead, sloped down to an edge that looked like a foot of granite.

Behind him, although he didn't know it, Kate Rashid mounted the circular stairs. Dillon took a deep breath and moved out into the rain, Walther extended. *Nothing.* He took another breath, and from above, the top of the cover over the door, Paul Rashid dropped on him, sending him to his knees. He chopped Dillon across the right wrist, so that he dropped the Walther. Dillon raised his elbow back into Rashid's face and managed to stand. He turned, and Rashid faced him, that magnificent uniform soaked in rain.

'Now then, my friend, at last.'

He launched himself at Dillon and they met breast-to-breast. Behind, the door opened and Kate appeared. She cried out as Rashid's greater weight forced Dillon back against the rail. There was a moment of struggle, then they went over together on to the leads, sliding apart.

The pouring rain had made the wet leads almost as slippery as ice. Rashid slid one way, lurched and went over the edge of the granite. Dillon slid a few yards away, but was more fortunate, his feet slamming against the granite.

He started to work his way along and held out a hand. 'Come on.'

'Go to hell.'

Down below, Joe Baxter and Billy looked up.

Dillon said. 'For God's sake, just take my hand and argue later.'

'No, damn you.'

There was a cry, and above them, Kate Rashid appeared. 'Paul, no.' She ducked under the rail and slid down the wet slope of the leads, finishing with her feet against the granite edge. Rashid was slipping further. She braced herself, reached and grabbed his left hand.

'Come on, Paul, just hang on to me.' He did for a

moment, and his weight pulled her forward so that she almost went headfirst over the edge.

He smiled up at her, nothing but love and understanding and a strange kind of grace, a most heartbreaking thing that would haunt her for the rest of her life.

'Hey, little sister, enough is enough. Not you, too.'

He pulled his hand free, almost floating away from her, turning over once in mid-air before hitting the terrace below beside Billy and Baxter.

There was no scream from her, nothing like that. It was as if every possibility of such a reaction had died for all time, such was the shock. Dillon caught her right hand and reached up for the first edge on the leads.

'Come on.' For a moment, she hesitated, and he tried again. 'Come on, unless you want to go, too.'

Something went out of her in a shuddering sigh, and he reached again, pulling them up to the railing.

She broke away from him and then ran down the stairs and through the Great Hall. Dillon picked up his coat and went after her. He paused on the steps and put the coat on her as she knelt over her brother. Billy, slightly dazed, and Baxter stood beside her. She looked up, her face incredibly calm.

'He's gone. You've done for all of them, Dillon, all my brothers.'

'I'm sorry.' It was the instinctive reply, empty and stupid.

'Go away.'

'For God's sake, girl.'

'This is my business, Dillon. Just go, you and your people. I'll deal with you later at a more suitable time.'

Dillon hesitated, then nodded to Baxter and Billy. 'Let's get out of it.'

They got in the Jaguar, Baxter started the engine and drove away. Dillon turned and looked. She was still kneeling.

'Are you all right?' he asked Billy.

'Sore as hell. What happened up there?'

'At the end, it was hand-to-hand. We fell across the rail, down the roof, and he went over. I offered my hand when he was hanging there, but he didn't want it. She slid down to join us, but he pulled away because he thought she'd go over, too.' When Dillon lit a cigarette, his hand shook. 'He said, "Hey, little sister, enough is enough. Not you, too."'

'Jesus Christ,' Billy said. 'What did she mean, I'll deal with you later at a more suitable time?'

'Simple, Billy, it means it's not over. Now I'd better phone Ferguson,' and he took out his mobile.

EPILOGUE

LONDON

To the world in general and the media in particular, it was a sensational story. That on a day of family tragedy, the funeral of two brothers, Paul Rashid, Earl of Loch Dhu and one of the richest men in the world, had fallen from the Angel Terrace of the Bell Tower at the ancient family home.

The sister's story had been simple. Leaving the reception after the funerals, he'd been distressed. He'd wanted to be alone and had gone up to the top of the Bell Tower, a favourite place. The stories were muted, the Rashids being who they were and having large holdings in both television and the newspaper world. Most newspapers spoke of a tragic accident, there was the odd hint of suicide, but that was all.

One story that was generally reported was the account of Paul Rashid's funeral. All the newspapers carried it. It was a simple service, not even the Dauncey villagers invited, an Imam from London joining the Rector, the only mourner Lady Kate Rashid. As usual, the media got it wrong, for someone else attended.

Sean Dillon didn't go into the church for the service. He sat with Billy in the Jaguar and waited.

'It's raining again,' Billy said.

'Nearly always does,' Dillon told him.

The cortège emerged from the church, Kate Rashid, now Countess of Loch Dhu, following behind the coffin. Dillon got out of the Jaguar.

Billy said, 'Do you want the umbrella?'

'What's a little rain, Billy?'

He let them reach the Dauncey family mausoleum, moved forward and stood at the edge of the churchyard while the Rector and the Imam did their thing. Strange, but Kate Rashid didn't have an umbrella and there was no one holding one over her. She stood in the rain, in her usual black, her only cover a black raincoat, while they took the coffin in. The Rector and the Imam shook hands, the undertakers dispersed.

She turned and started to walk away and came through the churchyard toward the gate where

Dillon stood. It was almost as if she moved in slow motion. She was totally alone, her dark hat shading her face, no emotion, not even when she got close to Dillon. It was as if he wasn't there – no, more, as if he didn't exist. She was so close that her coat almost touched him. She moved out of the gate and turned up the street toward Dauncey Place. Dillon watched her go, then returned to the Jaguar.

'Back to London.'

Billy started the car and drove away. 'Is that it, then?'

'I don't think so.'

On Friday night of that week, they met in the Dorchester Piano Bar, Harry and Billy, Ferguson and Dillon. Harry still wore a sling, Ferguson appeared normal, no sign of his broken arm. Dillon stepped behind the piano, lit a cigarette and started to play, working his way through a few standards. He was aware of her appearance but made no sign, continuing to play.

She leaned on the piano. 'I like that, Dillon. "A Foggy Day in London Town."'

'From *Damsel in Distress* – Fred Astaire.'

'I've seen the movie. Joan Fontaine was terrible, but you're good – good at everything.'

Seated at the end table, Ferguson and the Salters could hear the entire exchange. Dillon shook out another Marlboro and lit it with his old Zippo.

'What do you want, Kate?'

'Not just you, Dillon, you and your friends.'

She turned to the others and stood there in her usual black jumpsuit, only this one looked as if it had cost three thousand pounds at the Armani shop. Her black hair was superbly cut, hanging to her shoulders, and for once, she was ablaze with jewellery. She looked incredible, not just amazingly beautiful, but strong, powerful.

'The Queen of Sheba,' Dillon said quietly.

'Really?' she smiled.

'Oh, yes, and it's not just the Arab influence. There are Dauncey wives with marble faces from long ago in that church who have the same look.'

'You couldn't have paid me a greater compliment.'

Dillon slid from behind the piano and joined the group.

'Lady Loch Dhu,' Ferguson said formally, and they all stood.

'Sit, gentlemen.' They eased down. 'I thought

you'd like advance notice of today's news. American and Russian oil interests have agreed on terms for exploration in Hazar and the disputed Empty Quarter with Rashid Investments. There's been strong movement on the stock exchange for a family-owned firm, and me as Executive Chairman.' She smiled. 'Huge movements in New York and the City of London. We've jumped to seven billion. My accountants tell me it makes me the richest woman in the world.'

Ferguson managed a smile. 'Excellent, my dear.'

'I was sure you'd think that, General.'

There was silence. Dillon said, 'Get it done, Kate.'

She turned and actually smiled. 'Sorry, Dillon. I just wanted to say that I intend to destroy all of you. It's the Arab half of me, you see. I had three brothers, now I'm on my own.'

'And how do you intend to do it?' he asked gently.

'It doesn't really matter. I believe in the old saying that revenge is a dish best enjoyed cold. I can wait.' She smiled again. 'But it does leave you gentlemen on the dangerous edge of things. When you start the car, will it blow up? The footfall in the darkness, is it an assassin?'

'Do what you like, darling,' Harry Salter told her. 'People have been trying to knock me off for the last forty years.'

Ferguson said, 'My thanks for the advance warning. Very civilized.'

She smiled at Dillon. 'Don't forget me, Sean, and remember the Dauncey family motto: *I always return.*'

She walked away, supremely beautiful, the epitome of elegance.

Dillon watched her go and said softly, 'Oh, I won't forget you, girl.'